HELL'S INFERNO

(Joe Hawke #13)

Rob Jones

ISBN: 9781081907815

Other Books by Rob Jones

The Joe Hawke Series

The Vault of Poseidon (Joe Hawke #1)
Thunder God (Joe Hawke #2)
The Tomb of Eternity (Joe Hawke #3)
The Curse of Medusa (Joe Hawke #4)
Valhalla Gold (Joe Hawke #5)
The Aztec Prophecy (Joe Hawke #6)
The Secret of Atlantis (Joe Hawke #7)
The Lost City (Joe Hawke #8)
The Sword of Fire (Joe Hawke #9)
The King's Tomb (Joe Hawke #10)
Land of the Gods (Joe Hawke #11)
The Orpheus Legacy (Joe Hawke #12)
Hell's Inferno (Joe Hawke #13)

The Cairo Sloane Series

Plagues of the Seven Angels (Cairo Sloane #1)

The Raiders Series

The Raiders (The Raiders #1)

The Avalon Adventure Series

The Hunt for Shambhala (An Avalon Adventure #1)
Treasure of Babylon (An Avalon Adventure #2)

The Harry Bane Thriller Series

The Armageddon Protocol (A Harry Bane Thriller #1)

Website: www.robjonesnovels.com
Facebook: https://www.facebook.com/RobJonesNovels/
Twitter: @AuthorRobJones
Email: robjonesnovels@gmail.com

CHAPTER ONE

The man they called The Butcher reclined in the soft leather chair and sipped ice-cold vodka from a Russian shot glass.

He watched some scarlet macaws fighting in the top of a chonta tree just beyond his balcony and wondered which would win and prove his dominance over the other. He enjoyed the screeching and the growls and the claws and the feathers and the blood.

He enjoyed that sometimes there was a kill, the rarity of these events increasing the pleasure he took in them. He wondered what they would look like if he could only see them through ordinary glass instead of these tinted panes. Turning to the man standing in the shadows behind him, he snapped his fingers.

"Bring it."

The man stepped forward with a tray covered in a golden cloche. It sparkled in the twinkling light of the diamond chandelier above their heads.

"Serve it."

The man carefully set the tray down on the table beside the leather chair and removed the cloche to reveal a perfect steak tartare. It was presented on a golden plate and served with diced cornichons, chopped capers, fresh parsley and exquisitely sliced lemon cheeks. Sitting atop the raw beef was a single yellow egg yolk, unbroken, glossy and as raw as the bloody meat it garnished.

The Butcher studied it for a moment, almost hoping he could find a fault with the meal and have the servant horsewhipped for the trouble. But it was a delight, and a crocodile smile crept across his ghostly pale face. Leaning forward, he selected a spoon and popped open the yolk, scooping some of the slippery raw egg into his mouth and savoring the slimy texture before swallowing it.

He picked up a golden fork and used it to usher the trembling man back into the shadows.

"They eat so much clay it neutralizes the poison found in some of the berries they eat. Poison which would kill any other animal, but the scarlet macaw can gobble it up and live to tell the tale afterwards. A fascinating story, don't you think?"

The terrified man nodded in agreement. "Yes, sir, Mr Zamkov."

The Butcher skewered the raw grass-fed beef fillet and slid it into his mouth. "One man's meat is another man's poison." A moment passed; the silence was filled only with the sound of chewing. A tall, strong man in a crisp white shirt strolled into the room with his hands in his pockets. Tanned face, bright white teeth. Hair the color of raven's feathers slicked back with plenty of perfumed grease.

Zamkov snapped his fingers and the servant crawled away into the shadows, cringing his gratefulness as he went. Looking up at the new arrival, Zamkov swallowed the meat. "Is the American here yet?"

The man they called the Dove dipped his head to look at the chunky gold watch on his hairy wrist. Both hands remained in the pockets. "He arrived an hour ago."

Zamkov nodded. "Good. This will expedite the matter considerably."

"He seems nervous."

"Then he is smarter than he looks."

The Butcher drank more vodka and considered the smooth, cold taste of distilled wheat grain, and the subtle note of fresh green apples in the long, creamy finish. Pushing back into the sumptuous chair, he ran Eschaton through his mind for the thousandth time.

Eschaton.

The final event.

The end of the world.

A smile crawled over his face. This, he congratulated himself for, had been a long time coming, and he intended on enjoying it to the full. Others had been involved, foolishly trusting him and believing that they were part of the project when they were nothing but drones. Sergei Dimitrov and Joseph Kashala were two such men, working for him for what they thought was glory when they were working for nothing but their own destruction.

He had monitored the progress of the Bulgarian mafia chief and his squad of Congolese and Belgian mercenaries as they searched for Hades with interest. He had tracked their progress on his bank of monitors here in the compound. Kashala had reported total failure, and Dimitrov's death. If it was worth taking the Congolese general's life, he would have done it by now, but it wasn't. That would come soon enough.

There were countless others like Kashala all over the world, toiling away in the hope of being part of his glorious new world, when in fact they were just his slaves. If any of them had known the first thing about him, they would have broken ranks and betrayed him. Reported him to the authorities. Killed him. But they didn't know him.

No one did. Not even the Dove. None of them knew what he was capable of, but he did – only too well. As his hero had once said, a single death is a tragedy, but a million deaths is a statistic. Killing billions, in his case, was a statistic, but it was the single death that kept him up at night.

What he had done to that young woman in the apartment on Vernadsky Avenue.

His mind returned to the room and he realized his heart was tearing a hole in his chest. More vodka, *blink it away, Niki. Make it go away.*

He knew it never would. The look on her face. The sound of her screams. His heartbeat grew faster again. His mouth was dry and metallic and his eyes wide and staring, searching for something that might make it go away. The way she cried out.

The way she fought back.

He never even knew how it happened.

It just happened.

Only one thing could truly expunge the horror from his soul, and that was nothing less than the total destruction of mankind. Then, at last, he could live with the woman he had killed. The two of them alone, like Adam and Eve.

But she had to forgive him first.

"What do you want me to do?"

Zamkov was startled from his depraved reverie by the Dove's rich Caipira accent.

The reply, in contrast, was delivered in a cold, staccato Russian of western Moscow. "Make the American feel at home. Prepare the systems for display. Use the slaves in Sector 9."

"Consider it done."

Zamkov watched the Brazilian saunter back out of the room. He was the only person he had ever met who wasn't afraid of him, and he respected him for it. No one else had ever been able to maintain eye contact with him, or treat him as an equal.

Just the Dove.

And the woman from Vernadsky Avenue.

A shiver went down his spine as he finished the vodka and washed away the torment. Soon it would all be over. Soon it would be just the two of them.

Like Adam and Eve.

CHAPTER TWO

With nearly two full days on board the container ship, the ECHO team were more than grateful when they arrived in Tunis and stepped back on dry land. Their adventure in Istanbul was already just another mission in their pasts, and now their minds were focussed on tracking down Jackson Moran. Their friends were still imprisoned on Tartarus and only he knew its location.

Reaper's Tunisian friend, Youssef, met them in one of the city's teeming souks and walked them back to his home in the Ariana district. Stepping on the shaded cobblestones of yet another twisting alleyway, Lea closed her eyes and felt the warmth of the African city brush against her neck and shoulders.

The chaotic sounds of the Medina souk drifted to her ears. Sometimes she heard French and sometimes Arabic. They continued along the covered alley, the ruins of a Carthaginian palace in the distance giving the moment a timeless feel. Overhearing an argument, she opened her eyes and saw a salesman from one of the boutiques putting the hard sell on some tourists. Beside her, Ryan pointed out a stall selling local produce – mechouia salad, harissa and couscous. The smell of caraway, chilli and cumin floated on the hot, dry air.

Youssef pulled up to a stop beside a door covered in peeling blue paint. Somewhere in the distance the sound of a muezzin calling worshippers to prayer with the adhan rang out in the warm, fragrant air. Their host turned to them, glancing over their shoulders and spying down either end of the narrow cobblestone alley for any unwanted guests. "It's just through here my friends, and then we will be safe."

They followed him into a traditional Islamic courtyard and then up a set of stone steps until they reached a beautiful tiled rooftop garden. Potted fan palms ran around the outside of the garden and a single shezad seagrass lamp hung down from a wooden Arabic pergola. Youssef fussed around, repositioning chairs and plumping cushions.

"Please, have a seat. The water in the pitcher is mineral, from France. Bought just for you, as soon as I heard you were coming."

Reaper greedily eyed the chilled pitcher, covered in condensation and slapped him on the back. "Bien joué, mon ami."

They dumped their kit bags and tactical vests and all the rest of the gear they had fled Turkey with and slumped down on the soft chairs. The sun was high over the city and shining brightly on the blue and white houses of Sidi Bou Said, or what was once called Carthage, to the east. Here, on Youssef's roof under the shade, they were able to relax at last.

"And thank buggery for that," Scarlet said, stretching her arms and legs and yawning loudly.

"I think you speak for everyone," said Lea, sighing with relief as she sipped the iced water.

Hawke poured out a glass for himself and then swigged it down in one, wiping his mouth with the back of his filthy, dusty hand. "I'm praying you have a shower, Youssef?"

The Tunisian arms dealer nodded his head. "Of course. Perhaps you would prefer to clean up now and we can discuss business at dinner?"

A big, toothy grin appeared on Hawke's face. "You read my mind."

*

When they emerged back onto the roof after their showers, the sun was sinking and the western sky was streaked with red and orange ribbons, warm and soft as silk. The jumbles of whitewashed houses, flat-roofed and centred on cool, tiled courtyards were a softer amber color now. They stretched below them as far as the eye could see, cooling quietly in the evening twilight.

After a round of back-patting and laughs, Youssef invited everyone to sit and eat dinner. As they took in a table laden with chickpea soup, couscous, brik, Tunisian tajine and a great stack of khobz tabouna bread, Zeke whistled and slapped his stomach.

"It's a tough job," he said. "But someone's got to do it."

Ryan smacked a mosquito on his neck. "Can't we eat inside?"

Lea reached into her bag and threw him a small can of repellent. "Shut up and enjoy your food."

Youssef laughed. "Yes, and now we must also discuss the business at hand. Vincent told me you were trying to locate a man named Jackson Moran. He said you need him because of some information he has."

Lea nodded. "Yes. What can you tell us about him?"

"Jackson Moran is a senior officer with the US Defense Intelligence Agency, handling top-level defense contracts and other matters of the very highest national security classifications."

Lea said, "Our friend Orlando Sooke was able to track him down to Brazil, in the Amazon but…"

Youssef smiled. "But the Amazon is a big place."

"Exactly."

Hawke spoke up. "Reaper mentioned you might be able to help us make the Amazon a bit smaller?"

The Tunisian grinned. "It is already done, my friends. I put out some requests to my not inconsiderable arms dealing network and got some very interesting information back. Word on the black market is that Moran is meeting with a Russian named Nikita Zamkov, no less."

"No less?" Kamala said. "I never heard of her."

"It's a him," Youssef said. "But perhaps you know him by his other name – the Butcher."

She shrugged. "Still a no from me."

"The Butcher?" Lea asked. "Not getting great vibes from that name."

Ryan set down his fork. "The Butcher? Why do they call him that?"

Scarlet sighed. "Because he used to work on a delicatessen counter, why do you think?"

Ryan started chewing his dinner again and swallowed it. Ignoring her, he turned his eyes to Youssef. "Was he Mafia?"

"I don't think so. He's from Russia originally, somewhere out in Siberia. No one knows exactly where. No one knows anything much about him at all. Some say he was in the Russian Army, others say he was a king of the Moscow underworld." He shrugged. "And maybe he was both. I know nothing more about him, except he has a base somewhere in the Amazon basin, deep in the jungle away from the world's prying eyes. He calls is Vyraj."

"And what does that mean?" Lexi asked.

Youssef shrugged. "This is all I have."

"You know where we can find this Vyraj?" Lea said hopefully.

"No, but I know a man who knows a man."

"Sounds a bit ropey to me," Scarlet said.

Youssef sipped his mint tea. "I don't know *ropey*."

"She means it sounds very interesting," Lea said with a subtle scowl at her friend. "Who is this man who knows a man?"

"His name is Tiago Almeida. He moves from one filthy hole to another filthy hole in Europe, supplying guns to various clients across the continent. He spends most of his downtime in his hometown of Lisbon, and tells me he knows someone who used to fly people in and out of this mysterious base in the jungle. He has agreed to speak to you about it, for a price."

Lea rolled her eyes. "Of course, for a price."

"But is he reliable?" Hawke said flatly.

Their host raised his palms in a defensive gesture. "He is as reliable as anyone else in this business."

"That's not saying much," Scarlet said.

"All I can say is that I have dealt with him many times, and he has never let me down. I think you can trust him. I think the information he gives you will be good."

"And we're meeting him in Lisbon?" Lea asked.

Youssef shook his head. "He wants to meet you away from his hometown. He has chosen Gibraltar, and will meet you there tomorrow evening."

"Where and when, exactly?" Hawke asked.

"At sunset in the Sunborn Hotel."

"Fine. What about weapons?"

"I can furnish you with a wide range of weapons – this is my trade and I am the best in the world. Tell me, what sort of weapons do you want?"

"Yes," Scarlet said bluntly.

"Huh?

"All of the weapons," she said. "We want *all* of the weapons."

Lea rolled her eyes and gave the Tunisian a more specific list.

He listened carefully, then said, "I can get these for you."

"But how the hell are we going to get them to Brazil?" Lexi said. "Orlando's budget isn't stretching to a private jet all the way to Rio."

"You're flying with a commercial airline?" Youssef asked. "My condolences, but worry not, my friends. As I said, I am the best in the world. I will organize the weapons you choose to be ready for collection in Brazil. I have contacts everywhere."

"Thanks."

"For a price, naturally."

"For a price," Lea said.

Hawke finished his tea. "Naturally."

CHAPTER THREE

The Sunborn Hotel is a five star hotel set on board a superyacht moored in Gibraltar's Marina Bay. As Scarlet strolled along the sunset-soaked deck, she caught sight of the ship's casino and had to be pulled back into line by Hawke.

"Maybe later?" he said.

"Spoilsport."

With a cold beer in her hand, Lea stepped out of the bar and stopped dead on the deck. Ahead of her, the Rock of Gibraltar rose up in all its magnificence, lit orange and pink by the setting sun. The beauty of the moment almost took her breath away. She was here on the most unpleasant and time-critical of tasks – to get information from an arms supplier relating to the rescue of her friends on Tartarus – and yet for a few seconds her mind was whisked away to a better place.

Elysium.

She hadn't thought about the private island for a long time, but now she remembered the glorious sunsets over the Caribbean. The streams of pink light illuminating the royal palms running along the dunes of the western beach. The sounds of the royal terns and laughing gulls wheeling in the twilight. The sea turtles swimming over the offshore bar as she waded gently out to sea. The shape of the coral through the warm water.

It was paradise – their private paradise, but now nothing more than ruins guarded by the forces of President Faulkner. Like the others, she knew the only path home was to fight every inch of the way. Maybe then, she could turn her back on this life and start a new chapter with Hawke. Maybe, she thought fleetingly, start a family.

"Wow," Ryan said, lighting a cigarette. Shaking the match out and dumping it in a glass ashtray, he took a deep breath and exhaled. "This place is freaking awesome."

Lea pulled out a chair and sat down at the table. Hawke, Scarlet, Reaper and Ryan joined her while the others assembled at the poolside bar and enjoyed their drinks. The young Irishwoman scanned the busy bar for Youssef's contact but saw no one matching the description. All around her, smiling people were enjoying their evening, sipping drinks and reclining on the chic black deckchairs around the raised pool. One day, she thought, this will be my life.

"Head up," Ryan said. "If that's not our man, then I don't know my arse from my elbow."

Lea turned and watched a short, fat man step out onto the sun-baked deck. He raised his hand to his eyes to shield them from the sun and searched the poolside for them. A waiter obscured his view, and then he saw them.

When he reached the table, Tiago Almeida looked nervous. He took a seat. Sweat beaded on his forehead and his fingers drummed on the tabletop at a hundred beats per minute.

"You are Youssef's friends?"

Reaper gave a sullen nod. "I have known Youssef for many years."

"Thanks for agreeing to see us," Lea said.

Almeida shrugged. "I owed Youssef a big favor. This is the repayment."

"Must have been a big favor," she said.

"That is between Youssef and me."

Lea looked up at the famous Rock again, watched the sun sinking behind it and the day slowly turn to night. Some of the drinkers were moving inside to the covered bar area, but most were staying put, putting light jackets on and asking waiters to light the candles on their tables.

Hearing their innocent laughter and the simple pleasure they could take from sitting out sharing a few drinks with each other reminded her just how different her life was. She decided to shake the thought from her mind and move the conversation along. "He said you know about this Vyraj place?" she asked.

"Keep your voice down, for god's sake!" He glanced over both of his shoulders and then slunk down into his chair. "No one is supposed to know about it, and the Butcher has spies everywhere."

Hawke stopped drinking his beer and fixed laser-beam eyes on Almeida "Why do they call him the Butcher? Youssef was unclear."

"It's what they would call you if you had killed over ten thousand people in cold blood."

Scarlet was unfazed by the body count. It was certain to be a wild exaggeration, probably invented by the Butcher himself. "Killed ten thousand people? How did he manage that?"

Almeida shrugged. "Don't ask me. It's just what they call him, okay? Some say he killed those people just for sport out on the icefields in Siberia, but no one really knows. He is a recluse, and a maniac."

"And where can we find this Butcher and his little hidey hole?" Scarlet asked.

Almeida became distracted and shifted in his seat. "Before we go any further, you realize this is a business arrangement, right?"

"Yes." Lea's voice was flat and businesslike. She put her hand in her jacket and pulled out a small, brown envelope. "There's three thousand dollars in here."

"I asked Youssef for five."

Hawke leaned in and grabbed his tie, jerking his head down to the table. "But you're getting three because of the admin fee."

"Admin fee?"

"It's what I'm charging not to throw you over the side of this boat. All right?"

Almeida gave a nervous nod. "Sounds good to me. Very reasonable."

"Good."

As Hawke released him, the Portuguese man straightened his tie and glanced around to see if anyone had seen what Hawke had done. Content no one had, he leaned back in his seat and continued as if nothing had happened. He opened the envelope, counted the cash and slipped it inside his own jacket. Then he looked at Lea. "Unfortunately, I don't know where the Butcher can be found."

"Then you'd better give the cash back," Hawke said. "And get your water-wings on."

Lea held Hawke's arm back. "But Youssef said he knew a man who knew a man. So, who do *you* know?"

Almeida sighed and sipped his beer. "All right, it's true; I know a man who knows where you can find the Butcher."

"This is getting ridiculous," Scarlet said. "Youssef knows you and you know someone and he knows someone. This could go on forever."

"No," Almeida said. "Not forever. My contact's name is Dave Shorten. He's a Canadian bush pilot who cut his teeth putting out wildfires in British Columbia."

"And how do you know him?" Kamala asked.

"I know him from my travels in South America," Almeida said with a wry smile. "He became a friend. He got into poker but it turned out he was a very bad card player. Built up lots of debt and needed money fast. That was when he got the Amazon gig."

"For the money?" Lea asked.

"Pure and simple," Almeida said. "He was the best bush pilot on the market and that's how he came to the attention of Zamkov."

"So, the Russian hired him?"

Almeida sipped his beer and gave a nod. "As I say, he was a bush pilot. One of the best in the business, but after working for the Butcher for a few months he got spooked."

Lea set her drink down. "Got spooked?"

Almeida had raised the bottle to his lips and was downing the last of the chilled beer. He set the bottle down on the coaster and paused a beat. "He said he saw things."

"What kind of things?" Hawke asked.

A shrug. "He never elaborated. Whenever I asked him about it, he always changed the subject and refused to tell me anything further. I don't know what happened to him in the Amazon, but he was never the same man after he finally got out."

Lea felt the breeze brush her cheek. It was cooler now, and night was on the way. Her memories of Elysium had flown away into the approaching darkness without her even realizing it. She zipped her jacket up halfway and finished her drink. "Is this man still in Brazil?"

Almeida frowned. "Are you kidding? As soon as the Zamkov contract ended he got the hell out of there – not just the Amazon jungle but the entire country. There was no reason for him to hang around. He had the cash he needed to pay off his debts and set himself up for life."

"Where is he?" Ryan asked.

"He runs a bar on St. Lucia." Almeida handed Lea a piece of folded paper. "This is the address."

Hawke finished his beer. "That's all we needed to know, Tiago. Thanks."

"I have fulfilled my debt to Youssef, but I can't promise if the pilot will speak to you about this. He is a very private man, and he was terrified by some of the things he saw out in the jungle. He once told me he would never speak about it again, to anyone in this world."

Lea pushed her chair back and slipped the piece of paper into her pocket. "We'll see about that, and thanks for the beer."

CHAPTER FOUR

Lea Donovan slipped on her sunglasses and stared out into the dazzling St Lucia day. A white metal sun pitched down on them from directly above their heads. Cardinal blue sky and sparkling turquoise ocean. Heat rose in waves from the sandy beach and a steady breeze rustled the leaves of the palm trees.

"You okay?"

She turned to see Hawke standing beside her, aviator shades and a bright, honest smile. Even with the lines on his face, there was something eternally youthful and energetic about him.

"Sure, just reminds me of Elysium."

He nodded. "I know what you mean. We'll get back there."

"Maybe." She looked down the beach and saw a number of bars. "Which one do we want?"

"Any will do me," Scarlet said.

Zeke laughed. "Me too."

Taking Almeida's piece of paper from her pocket, Lea read the name he had written down and then glanced up at the beach bar. Hanging from a traditional palm thatch roof a few bars down the beach was a sign A RUM WITH A VIEW. Potted palms lined the outside edge of the veranda, and wooden steps led directly from the sand up into the cool shade of the bar's interior.

"A bit naff," Ryan said, looking at the hand-painted sign. "But if he has an ice-cold bottle of Singha in there somewhere, I'll let him off."

With her eyes obscured by her shades, Scarlet walked through the sand in a direct line toward the main bar. "It's heaven, but I'll leave the girly drinks to you. If this place doesn't have a chilled strawberry vodka daiquiri, I'll have your children."

Ryan's jaw flopped open. "Eh?"

Scarlet's laugh filled the air. "You're such a prat, Bale."

"I think I see Shorten," Camacho said, pointing. "Over there at the end of the bar, to the right of the barman."

"That's got to be him," Lexi said. "Matches Almeida's description perfectly."

Lea agreed. "Time to talk turkey, then."

"Can we trust him?" Reaper asked.

Ryan nodded. "According to my research, Almeida was telling the truth. He's an experienced bush pilot who commanded the respect of his colleagues. Before retiring he accrued tens of thousands of flying hours in single engine and twin-engine aircraft, and mostly in some of the most dangerous places on earth as far as flying planes goes – Indonesia, Nepal and finally Brazil. He packed it in after a close call in the Amazon and decided to cash everything out and buy this bar."

"And there you have it," Zeke said. "The man's entire resumé."

"We can't go in mob-handed," Hawke said. "Let me and Lea talk to him first."

"Fine with me," Lexi said, eying up the barman. "I could use a cold drink and some time out with that guy."

"Oh *please*," Ryan said. "He's a walking cliché – tall, dark, handsome. What has he got that I haven't?"

"The next ten minutes of my time," Lexi said with a wink.

Leaving the laughter behind, Hawke and Lea approached the older man at the end of the bar.

"You can get served down there, folks," he said cheerfully.

"Are you Dave Shorten?"

He set his beer bottle down and narrowed his eyes. "Who wants to know?"

"We talked to Tiago Almeida in Gibraltar, sir," Lea began. "We know all about your work in Brazil."

"I never worked in Brazil and I never knew anyone called Almeida."

"That's funny." Hawke pulled up a stool, metal legs scraping on the hardwood floorboards. "Because he seemed to know all about you, from the pilot gig in the Amazon all the way down the line to the poker debts."

Shorten glanced down the bar and hushed him with a downward movement of his hands. "Hey, take it easy, will you? No one here knows about that part of my life."

"And yet we do," Lea said coolly. "Ready to talk about Almeida now?"

"Almeida yes, but Brazil not any time soon. No one should have to see what I saw in that god-forsaken place, and if it's all right with you, I'd rather not revisit it ever again, even just in my mind."

"It's not all right with us," Hawke said, slowly losing his patience. "Some very good friends of ours are in a lot of trouble, and the only man who can give us the information we need to help them is currently a guest at Zamkov's little playhouse in the jungle."

"You know Zamkov's name?"

"We know a lot more than that," Lea said, sipping her beer. "But what we don't know is where his base is located. Tiago Almeida told us you'd seen things, terrible things that you don't like to talk about."

"Yea, I saw some stuff, and let me tell you what they say is true. Some things cannot be unseen."

"Go on."

"Maybe you didn't understand Tiago because of the Portuguese accent, so let me give it to you in a Canadian one – I don't like to talk about it."

Lea pulled out a wad of one hundred dollar bills. "Consider it a tip for the great service."

Shorten flicked through the cash and pocketed it. "Okay. For one thing, it ain't no goddam playhouse. The place is like something out of a James Bond film. It's built on top of one of the tepui mesas and surrounded by layers of security. You know he has launchpads there, right?"

When she heard that, Lea was unsure what to say next. "At this point in time, we know only what you tell us about the place."

Scarlet and Ryan walked over, drinks in hand. "How's it going?" Scarlet asked.

Shorten nudged his chin at the new arrivals. "Who are they?"

"They're with us," Hawke said.

"So, you're the guy who got spooked?" Ryan asked.

Shorten rounded on them. "Listen, I'm no coward and I won't sit here and let anyone tell me I'm one, understand?"

Ryan backed down. "I'm sorry. I didn't mean anything by it."

"Please excuse our monkey," Scarlet said. "He's uncomfortable in human company."

"Hey!"

"Listen, you don't know what you're messing with here," Short said darkly as he lit a cigarette. "You've heard the phrase playing with fire?"

"Of course."

"This is worse than that, this is playing with an inferno, specifically Hell's Inferno."

Lea and Hawke exchanged a look, and then the rest of the team meandered over, cold beer bottles in hand and sunglasses perched on foreheads.

"Don't tell me," Shorten said. "These are all friends of yours, too?"

"You got it in one," Hawke said. "You can trust all of them."

Lea sipped her beer, still enjoying the warm breeze blowing through the open bar. "You mentioned something called Hell's Inferno. What does that mean, exactly?"

"The locals call the area *A Fornalha do Inferno*. Translated literally it means the furnace of hell, but English speakers call it Hell's Inferno." He sucked hard on his cigarette until the embers began to burn into the filter. Wincing, he blew out the acrid smoke and with trembling, nicotine-stained fingers he stubbed it out in the upturned beer cap. "It's the very worst place on earth."

Scarlet frowned. "I thought that was…"

"Hold it." Lea raised her hand. "Wherever you're about to say just isn't going to be funny."

"Spoilsport."

"This is no time for jokes," Shorten said, lighting another cigarette. "If you're seriously considering going into that place, you'd better leave your sense of humor right here on this island."

"We're sorry," Lea said, steering things back to business. "Mr Almeida told us you were hired by Zamkov to fly people in and out of the compound."

"That's right. I flew people in and out of there for weeks. They rarely spoke, but I got the impression they were scientists of some kind. Serious dudes with long faces. The kind of guys who pack their vacation stuff in diecast aluminum boxes, if you catch my drift. Boxes with ESCHATON stencilled on the side."

Hawke and Lea caught each other's eye again, behind them, Lexi drank some beer. "Sounds interesting."

"Or dangerous," Kamala muttered.

Shorten looked at the former Secret Service agent and then at Lexi. "You should listen to your friend. She's smart. Dangerous doesn't begin to describe what you'll find in that jungle."

"Elaborate," Scarlet said coolly.

"You have a real way with words, you know that?"

"So I'm told."

He sighed. "A few times from the air, I saw what can only be described as a hunt."

"Hunting has been illegal in Brazil since 1967," Ryan said.

"Yeah," Shorten drawled. "Hunting *animals*, but we're not talking about going on a boar shoot or nothing like that."

"Zamkov hunts people?"

Shorten gave a dry, bitter laugh. "Zamkov never leaves the compound, so no."

"I know what's going on," Lexi said with disgust. "He hires the place out to rich businessmen and they come in and hunt people."

Shorten shook his head. "Nothing as common as that. Hell, *that* goes on all over the goddam world. Oh, no. Nothing like that for the Butcher."

"Then what?" Lea asked.

"Mr Zamkov tests his weapons systems on people out in the jungle." He took a long pull on the beer and drained the bottle dry. "That's what."

A long, grim silence hung over the team like a black veil.

The sombre Russian monk was first to break the silence. "Ёшкин кот!"

Only Ryan understood what he had said. "I'll see your *damn it* and raise you a get out of here."

"He tests weapons systems on human beings?" Camacho said.

Kamala put her beer down. "That's the most disgusting thing I ever heard."

"You should hear Ryan in the bathroom," Scarlet said. When everyone turned to look at her, she shrugged. "Hey, it's how I deal with shit like people being used as target practice."

Hawke's face had grown much more serious since hearing about the human targets. "All right, what else can you tell us about this compound?"

"I never got a great view of it from the air," he said quickly. "The ATC always brought us in from the east, and always down nice and low. By the time we reached the place the wheels on the bottom of the Caravan were practically brushing the canopy. I only ever saw the runway and the ATC tower from the air, and that crazy spherical building in the middle. That's the nerve center."

Reaper lit up a cigarette and waved out his match. "And what about on foot?"

"Not much. I never had clearance to leave the airfield. The guys I dropped off and picked up used to leave the terminal and climb into little golf carts. They drove off into the main compound and that was that, but there were other rumors."

"Go on."

He inhaled the smoke and stared out across the ocean. Lea could see herself in the reflection of his mirror sunglasses.

"Rumors about experiments. It was when I started to hear about the experiments, I knew it was time to back off and stop flying there."

"Experiments?" Lea asked.

He nodded gravely. "That's what they say. Real nasty stuff. You got to remember, he's as rich as a man can be. No one knows exactly how much money he has – it's all parked in shell companies and tax havens. But if you ask me, he's not just sitting down there in the jungle burning up millions of dollars every year for fun. He's planning something real big and when it goes down the whole world's gonna shake."

"But what do you mean when you say experiments?" Ryan asked.

"Stuff with technology. Real sick stuff. Some say he turns people into cyborgs."

"My God."

"And you know how everyone's wetting their pants about getting upgraded to 5G? Yeah, fuck that, because Zamkov is at least 10G."

"Holy crap," Lea said. "Imagine that in the hands of a psycho."

"I don't think's he a psycho, exactly, but he *does* have some sort of psychiatric condition, at least that's what the rumors were."

"Like what?"

He shrugged. "No idea, but I don't think he's a psychopath. He has a Yes Man though, and the goon is a different story. They call him *O Pombo*. It means The Dove in Portuguese. It's a sick contortion of reality because he's the least peaceful man and coldest psycho you will ever meet."

"Hmm." Scarlet put a black-painted fingernail to her lip. "The Butcher and the Dove. Sounds like a great double act."

"Yeah," Zeke said. "Look out Laurel and Hardy."

"I was thinking the Hawke and the Dove," Lea said. "And I know who my money's on."

Ryan frowned. "Seriously? You'd bet against Joe? I thought better of you."

Lea ignored him. Her mind was still on what Shorten had just said. "You're sure about the 10G thing?"

"As sure as shit."

She gave a low whistle. "Now I've heard it all."

Shorten gave her a look. "You'd think."

"And what does that mean?"

"It means his talents are not limited to weapons technology. Some of the men I flew in and out used to talk in the back of the plane. I don't think this was allowed, but they did it all the same. From what I can gather, Zamkov also dabbles in biowarfare projects. They also said he had residential and industrial property all over the world, so who knows where else this shit is going down?"

"I want you guys to know, right now," Zeke said with a smile, "that when you get back from the compound, I'll be right here in this bar. Good luck to y'all."

"Our Texan friend has the right idea," Shorten said. "If I were you guys, I'd stay as far away from the place as you can get."

"That's not an option," Hawke said. "We need to make contact with someone at the base."

"Listen," Shorten said wearily. "Stay away. They call him the Butcher, and with good reason, believe me. To say he's somewhere out on the antisocial personality disorder spectrum is the understatement of the century. Most on the base were too scared to say anything about him at all. It was like he was some sort of god who could see and hear everything that went on at the compound. Workers were terrified to say too much in case it got back to him, and he has a surface-to-air missile defense system and elite guards on the mesa's cliffs, too."

"Fair enough," Scarlet said. "Who hasn't these days?"

Shorten was unmoved by the attempt at humor. "He doesn't deal with traitors or slackers too kindly, and if I didn't mention it before, he tests high-tech weapons out on human beings. Stay away."

Hawke had heard enough. Setting his beer down for the last time, he fixed his eyes on the bush pilot and lowered his voice. "Where is this compound, exactly?"

Shorten laughed. "You're not serious? After all I just said?"

Lea peered up at Hawke and then stared at Shorten. "Yeah, that's his serious face. You'd better tell him where the compound is located before he puts on his angry face."

The Canadian bush pilot looked at them, shook his head, sighed and pulled a piece of paper out from behind the cash register. "It's your funeral." Handing Lea the paper, he took another sip of his beer and put his feet back up on the table. "And those coordinates did *not* come from me."

CHAPTER FIVE

The terrified woman watched Zamkov gnawing at the raw meat and nearly threw up. Just watching the bloody cuts of steak slide into his mouth made her stomach turn over and she had to fight hard to keep its contents where they were. Like many others here in Hell's Inferno she had heard the rumors about his eating habits, but seeing it up front and for real was another thing altogether.

His ghostly-pale hands ripped the meat in two and pushed another piece over his blood-stained teeth. He sounded like he was enjoying it more than might be expected, too. The red blood ran over his fingers and hands as he rummaged around in the bowl for more. "This is good, Adriana," he muttered in his thick Russian accent. "This is very good. I am impressed. You have sourced very good quality meats."

Urgently, she found something else to look at. In this case, it was the hot wind blowing through the lupuna trees outside the tinted windows. "Thank you, Mr Zamkov, sir."

He mumbled a response and stuffed more of the meat into his mouth. "Some don't understand how I do this, but if only they knew how good it tasted. Once you try it, you can never go back."

He held a piece out to her and she looked at it momentarily. Limp, red, soft and blood seeping from the sinews. Unable to find words, she shook her head and smiled.

"It's so smooth," he purred. "It just slides down."

She wondered how he had survived all these years eating like this. She thought about the bacteria and other diseases he risked consuming, but he showed no concern. Rumors had it he was practically a carnivore, but some said they had seen him eating raw eggs and others even said they had watched him eat the occasional salad as a garnish.

Did that make him a carnivore? She didn't know.

Looking up at the wall of monitors, he finished the meat and rubbed his mouth with a freshly laundered white napkin. He tossed the blood-streaked cloth to the table beside the bowl and clicked his fingers to get her attention.

"Sir?"

"The Dove is waiting outside. Show him in."

"Sir."

The Brazilian hitman strolled back into the room, hands in pockets. "You called?"

"How did the meeting go?"

"They are not prepared to meet your price."

Zamkov squeezed the arms of his leather seat, but then relaxed his fingers. The Chinese defense contractors waiting down in the conference room had made a foolish decision not to accept the terms of the deal he had proposed to them.

"And that's their final decision?"

The Dove nodded. "They say the aerial systems are affordable, but the land-based systems are too expensive."

"Don't they realize what research and development went into those?"

The tall Brazilian gave a shallow shrug. The truth was he didn't know the first thing about Zamkov's technology, and both men knew it.

The Russian sighed. "In that case, make sure our guests are shown my full hospitality."

"Yes, sir, of course."

"I wouldn't want them leaving here saying bad things about me. In fact, I don't want them leaving here at all. Do you understand?"

He nodded. "Yes, sir."

Zamkov closed his eyes and imagined the smug self-satisfied faces of the Chinese officials as the Dove dumped them on the banks of the *Rio do Fogo*, the River of Fire. He smiled as he saw them in his mind, standing in the jungle in their suits, a deep confusion etched on those very same faces. As for when they were introduced to the systems they had dismissed as overpriced… some things in this world were priceless. He would be enjoying the whole show on his monitors.

"The jungle is a big place," he said at last. "And Hell's Inferno is the very worst of it, especially if you're not welcome here."

"I understand."

The Dove slowly walked back out of the vast space of mission control. When he was halfway across the shining, polished concrete floor, Zamkov called out to him. "Have you seen Valentina, today?"

A long, uncertain pause. "No, sir. I thought she was in the lab."

"I asked her to visit me," he said sadly. "I don't think she's ready to talk to me yet, not after what happened."

The woman looked from Zamkov up to the Dove. He had the looks of a supermodel, but from what she had seen, the mind of a wild animal. Now, he seemed to be thinking carefully about what to say next, which was very unlike his usual, calm, confident manner.

"I'm sure she is," he said at last. "She's probably just too busy. There's a lot to learn in a place like this."

"Yes, you're right. Of course. You may go."

The Dove turned and vanished into the labyrinthine compound, and Zamkov nodded and mumbled to himself and walked over to the window. "Soon this will be the only safe place in the world, Adriana. Think about that. Think about how lucky we all are."

So, he was really going to go through with it, she thought. She felt a shiver go up her spine as she imagined the destructive power of Project Eschaton when it was finally unleashed on the human race.

"Yes, sir."

"You are dismissed."

She bowed and stepped away from him. The words *eschaton* and *unleased on the human race* were still echoing in her mind as she drew closer to the door. Pausing there, she just caught sight of one of Zamkov's helicopters as it began to make its descent above the River of Fire. In the back were the Chinese defense contractors.

"This is going to be one hell of a show, Adriana!"

"Yes, sir," she said, a desperate, cold fear for her life choking back what she really wanted to say to him.

"Their only escape is by the river, but it's nearly at boiling point! Will they choose to die at the hands of my robots, or boil themselves to death?"

As Zamkov laughed and clapped his hands in joy, she turned away, leaving the Butcher in front of his monitor bank, his fingers now dipping into the bowl of raw beef strips on the table beside him.

CHAPTER SIX

Alex ran her tongue around the gap where her tooth used to be and winced in pain. Mr Mahoe had been as good as his word, and he'd set to work as soon as the soldiers had strapped her down to the gurney in his torture chamber.

The pain was excruciating, but he was a true master of his art. When he dropped the tooth down in the bowl, it landed with a sharp tinkling sound, and then he put down the pliers. He told her to go back to her cell and contemplate the situation for a day or two, because the next time they met he would be extracting every last tooth in her mouth.

And like with the first one, there would be no anaesthetic.

The hole felt much bigger than it really was, and her swollen, torn gums were only just beginning to heal. The copper zing of blood still flooded her mouth and she found it almost impossible to eat the slop they brought her without pain radiating through her head.

The agony was real, and hard, and when she thought about that monster ripping out every tooth in her mouth, the terror of it made her feel like throwing up. Would he really go through with it? Yes, she had no doubt. That bastard Blanchard was probably going to watch through the two-way mirror at the end of Mahoe's squalid little room.

If only she could speak to her father, or even Brandon McGee. Had Mahoe worked on them, too? Maybe he had gone further and they were dead? Worsened by the pain and lack of sleep, her imagination turned into a maelstrom in her mind and almost drove her crazy. She had tortured visions of Faulkner forcing her father into some sort of kangaroo court – a hideous show trial designed to humiliate him – and then finding him guilty of treason.

And what frightened her most was that Faulkner would use *her* as leverage to get the confession he needed. That thought was nearly as terrifying as the idea of her second appointment with Mr Mahoe. That's what the sadistic bastard had called it – an appointment.

She felt sick when she thought about it, and when she heard someone fumbling with a key to the lock on her cell door, her stomach did a somersault. Maybe next time, Mahoe would go all the way and kill her. Her hands started to shake, her mouth went dry and the room began to spin around her. In blurred motion, she saw the cell window, the metal sink, the concrete floor, and she thought she was going to faint.

And then she saw Brandon McGee.

He was standing in the doorway, the chunky key to her door held in a hand crowned with split, bleeding knuckles.

"Brandon? Is it really you?"

"Yes, and we need to get out of— are you okay? You look like you're going to throw up."

"I thought they were taking me to see Mahoe."

"Who the hell is Mahoe?"

"You mean you two haven't been introduced?"

"No, but we can talk about it later. Let me help you into the chair."

When she was sitting in it, he clicked off the brakes and steered her to the open door. For a wild moment, Alex thought she was dreaming and that any second, she was going to wake up and find herself looking up at Mahoe. Just thinking about that tattooed psychopath made her shudder, but maybe now she would never see him again.

"How the hell did you escape?"

Brandon performed a neat three-sixty turn by the door so they were going backwards now, with him stepping out into the corridor first. He pulled his torn suit jacket back and she saw the grip of a handgun stuffed down the waistband of his pants. Drawing it, the Secret Service agent pulled back the slide and pointed the muzzle at the floor as he craned his neck around the cell door.

"Clear," he said, and she saw now it was a Beretta M9, the standard sidearm of the US military.

"I'm guessing someone didn't just hand that over to you?"

He reversed into the corridor and spun around once again so she was in front. "You guessed right. I disarmed one of the guards when they came into my cell."

"Did you kill them?"

"What do you think?"

"Sorry I asked."

"I had no choice. You get half a chance in a situation like this and you grab it with both hands. We're prisoners here, Alex and it's our duty to rescue the president and do everything we can to escape and get him to safety."

Alex felt her heart quicken. "You mean he's alive?"

"So the guard told me, yes."

"Do you know where they're keeping him?"

"He told me the prison section of the base is divided into four quarters. I was in Q4, we're in Q2 right now. He said your father is in Q1, but he was under duress at the time."

Alex felt a wave of relief wash over her. Since they had been separated, the terrible fear lurking at the back of every thought was that they had executed her father, or that he had been shot and killed trying to fight back or escape. At least now she knew he was safe, and that they had a shot at getting out of here.

"Did the guard tell you how to get to Q1?"

"Yes, it's to the east of this location, but we're going to have to work fast. When they discover those two dead guards in my cell, all hell is going to break lose around here."

Alex's initial excitement was starting to tarnish. Brandon had got her out of her cell and they knew her father was still alive, and his location, but they were still on Tartarus. None of them had any idea where that was, or how to get away from the place. What if there were thousands of soldiers here, all ordered to keep them on the base?

Brandon seemed to read her mind. "I'm not going to lie to you, Alex – this is a very shitty situation right now. All my training and experience is telling me we have no chance at all."

"We can do it, Brandon. We have to."

"I hope you're right – you have your father's spirit. But things are bad."

And then they got worse when a loud klaxon started blaring throughout the facility.

"Looks like they found the guards," he said.

"Damn it! They'll probably move dad to a more secure location."

Brandon gripped the wheelchair's push-handles tighter and started running for the door at the end of the corridor. "Then we'll just have to work faster. Hold on, Alex – this could get rough!"

"Don't worry, I'm holding on," she said, her heart beating hard in her chest.

Holding on for my life.

CHAPTER SEVEN

ECHO touched down on the tarmac just as the sun was setting over the Amazon rainforest. The commercial Air France flight from Lisbon to Tefé offered no more excitement than the two changes at Paris and São Paulo. From there, they took a domestic flight north into the Amazon jungle, landing just before full night.

The airport at Tefé was one of the most remote in Brazil, but the city was the largest commercial hub in the Solimões region. The Portuguese had settled this place four hundred years ago in 1620 but the native Muras people had lived here for countless centuries before. Today, the city was the main departure point for tourists journeying into the Mamirauá Reserve, a vast expanse of wetlands and flooded rainforest four times bigger than Luxembourg.

Despite this, life was in a low gear when the team stepped down out of the aircraft and walked across the tarmac in the evening twilight. Thanks to a covert logistics chain stretching back to Sir Richard Eden via Chris Raynes and Orlando Sooke, they were met by a local man and former soldier who had been introduced to them only as Pedro.

Behind him loomed the neat, slick silhouette of an Airbus Panther, a twin-engine military helicopter. When they got closer Hawke saw all the previous military insignia had been painted over with plain olive green to match the rest of the aircraft. His eyes crawled over some vehicles behind the chopper and a row of squat airport buildings in the distance. Forgetting about the sniper who had killed valuable team members, just because they were in such a remote location, was not a mistake a man with his experience would make.

Lea stepped up. "Pedro?"

A short, squat man with a scar running down the left side of a stubbly chin, Pedro seemed anxious and keen to get things over with. His eyes danced over the foreign team and flitted along the line of windows on the airport terminal behind them, as if he were looking for some kind of threat. In response to Lea, he stepped out of the chopper's shadow. "Sim… *yes*."

"It's good to meet you."

"You want to go west into the jungle." It was a statement, not a question.

"Yes, on the Amazon River," Lea said, handing him Shorten's handwritten coordinates. "Here. What about the weapons?"

"In the chopper. We must hurry. Please, climb on board and I will start the engine."

Lea looked at Hawke. He shrugged in response. "Maybe he likes an early night?"

"Get in the helicopter, you idiot."

Hawke laughed, but his mind was in a more serious place. When the team were all inside and buckled up, and the chopper was racing west above the jungle canopy, he turned his attention to the nuts and bolts of the mission. Working as an operative in the SBS meant being able get the hardest of jobs done either alone or in a small team, but his previous existence as a major in the Royal Marines Commandos had given him solid experience in leading larger teams and serious strategic planning.

Since finding out the location from Shorten back in St. Lucia, he had asked Ryan to try and get into Zamkov's life from the Brazilian angle. Except for a brutal murder he was believed to have committed while at university, his Russian life was mostly a mystery, but with a footprint as big as his, there had to be a trail of breadcrumbs leading from the compound back to the authorities in Brasilia.

The bush pilot had told them that the Butcher had private residential compounds in many countries, but Ryan had dug up some new information. According to his research, the Brazilian Government had played hardball before giving Zamkov permission to construct his largest and most impressive base of all – right here in the jungle. Rumors about bribes and blackmail swirled like a maelstrom, and if what Shorten had said about the dangerous Russian was true, Hawke had no trouble believing them.

What worried him more was why he wanted to build his new criminal empire hub out here in the world's most remote location. The ECHO team's chief concern was securing Jackson Moran from the compound and extracting the location of Tartarus from him. Only that way did they stand a chance of rescuing Alex, President Brooke and Brandon McGee, but he knew there was another reason why the Butcher was out here in this part of the jungle and he wanted to know why.

When Scarlet broke the silence, her voice was thin and weak over the chopper's internal comms. "Something tells me this mission is going to be about a hell of a lot more than getting Moran to squeal."

"Me too," Hawke said. "Call me crazy, but when a Russian criminal underworld kingpin buys millions of acres of Amazonian rainforest and builds a complex the size of a space center on it, I get nervous."

"You're not crazy," Ryan said. "I did what you asked and looked into the compound itself – to try and get some solid data rather than the hearsay of drunken bush pilots, and the further you go the nastier it gets."

"How so?" Lea asked.

"I hacked the Brazilian Government's planning portal for this state and located the application and plans for the compound."

Reaper fired up a cigarette and blew the smoke out the open door. "What did you find?"

"The whole thing was handled by a team of Brazilian architects called Projeto 19, or Project 19. They're based in Rio and from what I can tell, they're totally above board and on the level."

Lea said, "Unlike the Butcher."

"Unlike the Butcher," Ryan repeated. "And the plans are terrifying. The place is basically a hidden lair about the same size as a small international airport, with dozens of buildings all connected by glass walkways. It's all ultramodern in design and according to the plans, there are several laboratories in the centre of the compound, with residential buildings around the outside."

Hawke whistled. "And the security?"

Ryan gave an apologetic shrug. "These are architectural drawings, so that sort of information isn't here, but I can say that there are specific guardhouses at all the entrances and a lot of residential units, so my guess is there are a lot of security guards."

Scarlet also lit a cigarette and passed the lighter back to the Frenchman. Slowly exhaling a thick stream of smoke, she sighed and said, "Got to feel sorry for them really. They have no idea what's about to hit them."

"And we have no idea what's about to hit us," Hawke said. "When I hear the words laboratories and hidden lair and biowarfare in the same briefing, I don't get good vibes."

Reaper gave a sage murmur of agreement. "Whatever we find in that place, it will not be good, mes amis. We must be ready for the very worst."

"Reap's right," Lea said. "Getting Moran is our priority, but if there's any other shit going down in that place, then we have a duty to put an end to it."

"Like buggery do we," Scarlet said. "Beyond Moran, all we have is hearsay. I say we just get in, get our man, and get out. Simple as that. If we go chasing whatever the hell we find in there, we might never come out again, and right now Alex and her father need us… the whole world needs us. We can't leave a man like Faulkner in the White House and only we can bring him down. And what about Rich? He needs us, too. As long as that arsehole's in the White House, he's under house arrest."

All eyes turned to Hawke. While they were talking, he had given the matter some thought. "I'm sorry, Cairo, but I agree with Lea. We don't know what the Butcher's been up to, but I know one thing – I couldn't live with myself if I walked away from any kind of evil. If he's been using the compound for anything illegal or unethical, I have to put a stop to it and then call the authorities in to finish the job."

"Great," Scarlet said. "Now you're going to advertise our presence to the Brazilian Government – why not just send Faulkner an embossed invitation asking him to send some Special Ops over to our next motel?"

He made a face at her. "We'll be long gone by the time we contact the authorities, as you well know."

Lea doubled down on Hawke's point. "We'll get to Faulkner, Cairo, but we have to live with ourselves along the way, yeah? And don't worry about Rich – he'll be knocking back dry sherries down the Special Forces Club in no time."

"You talked me into it,' Scarlet said, softening her tone. "It must have been the word *sherries*."

Everyone laughed, except Ryan. He had already tuned out of the conversation and turned his thoughts to just how far he had come since meeting his new friends. Sitting in the open door of the chopper, legs hanging out and feet resting on the landing skid, he reflected on the winding journey his life had taken over the past few years. He lit the cannabis joint and leaned back against the metal door. From a no hoper computer hacker in a London squat, to skimming over the canopy of the Amazon in a stolen helicopter. Some journey.

He sucked in the dope and blew it back out into the steamy air. The *whomp whomp whomp* of the rotors above his head punctuated his thoughts and the downdraft ruffled his hair. He considered his new fugitive status and laughed. None of it mattered. He was here with the best friends he had ever known and for the first time in years, he felt like he could really breathe.

No, these people were more than friends.

They were family.

Joe Hawke at the helm, piloting the team through the madness and Lea Donovan charting the course with her conscience. He turned and looked at them now.

Vincent Reno smoking a roll-up cigarette and stripping his gun. Lexi Zhang staring out across the endless wilderness through her aviator shades.

Scarlet Sloane sitting with her head pushed back in her seat and her eyes closed, no doubt dreaming of her private island. Jack Camacho sitting beside her, also with his eyes closed, and their hands clasped together.

And the newest members. Zeke, Kolya and Kamala. Huddled together at the back of the chopper's cabin they talked in hushed tones, probably still in shock at what their lives had become.

He dragged once again on the joint and enjoyed the sensation of the cannabis smoke hitting his bloodstream as his thoughts drifted to the fallen.

Sophie Durand.

Bradley Karlsson.

Olivia Hart.

Maria Kurikova.

Danny Devlin.

Kim Taylor.

The list went on.

A long line of fallen friends, receding into the past now. Sometimes he went days without thinking about any of them, including even his beloved Masha. And who decided who lived and died, anyway? None of those men and women knew they were going to die when they stepped up to the plate and went on their last missions. Maybe this would be his last mission.

He didn't know and it didn't matter. Not anymore. All that mattered now was the moment, the here and the now, the present tense. Maybe a rocket would come screeching out of a clearing just ahead of them and blow them all to pieces in a few seconds. Maybe when they landed, it would be a trap and they'd be slaughtered in a bloodbath of automatic gunfire.

Just no way to know.

He looked up through the whirring blades. A quicksilver moon brushed long streaks of high clouds with white light. *What a crazy life*, he thought.

He dragged on the cigarette and laughed. The cannabis was going to his head just when he needed his head most of all. He stubbed it out on the stainless steel door frame and flicked it out into the great green nowhere. Somewhere out there, all hell was about to break loose, and he was going to find himself right bang-smack in the middle of it.

Just where he wanted to be.

CHAPTER EIGHT

In the deep Brazilian night, the Panther swooped down into a meander on the Amazon River's north bank. Hawke and the rest of the ECHO team knew what they had to do. When the chopper touched down in a small clearing, they streamed out one by one. Boots smacked down on the wet ground as they all jogged away from the whirring blades.

Hawke spoke into his mic and told Pedro they were all clear. The blades whirred faster as the helicopter powered up and climbed above the tops of the tropical plants surrounding the clearing. The Panther's engine grew fainter as the chopper pulled away to the east, leaving them alone in the jungle. It was hot. Clothes stuck to their sweat-soaked skin and the chorus of rainforest insects raged in the darkness.

Ryan hefted his bag off the ground and slung it over his shoulder. "Welcome to the jungle."

A groan.

"C'mon! Someone had to say it!"

"And that someone just had to be you, didn't it?" Scarlet said. "Tit."

Hawke lifted the night vision monocular to his eyes and scanned the undergrowth for any signs of life. In the darkness of the jungle night, nothing moved. "Looks like we're alone."

"Time to get moving," Lea said. "We need to get to the compound before daylight."

Weapons loaded and bags over shoulders, the team checked their compasses and located south by southwest. Reaper stared up at the sky, tracking the position of the constellations before striking out. "You are never lost on a clear night."

Kamala slipped her arms through the shoulder straps of her backpack and hefted it up on her back. "Anyone see the mesa?"

"It should be west of current position," Hawke said. "Got it!"

"Me too," Scarlet said. "It's mostly obscured by the trees."

Hawke slipped the monocular into his pocket. "We'll get a better view when we get closer. Let's get moving. We'll march through the night and split up at dawn to attack on two fronts."

"Sounds like a plan," Lea said.

Ryan soon learned it was one thing to suggest marching through the night, but another thing altogether to do it. Two hours into the trek, he had blisters on his shoulders from the pack on his back and on his heels and ankles from his boots. He guessed everyone else did too, but he didn't want to moan about it in case they didn't, so he decided to wait until they pulled up for rest before tending to them.

As the night grew darker, so too did their legs grow weary. The heat and humidity were ruthless allies in the war against anyone foolish enough to enter this place, and they were all feeling the punishment. They stopped for food and water, filling hungry stomachs and slaking desperate thirsts, and then marched again, walking along the northern edge of an impressive tree-filled canyon. They stopped a second time. More water and a compass check before changing their course ten degrees to the south.

In the sticky darkness, Hawke raised his hand and halted the team in a small clearing.

"What is it?" Lea asked.

"I hear something."

"Where?"

"There!"

It was too late. Men in jungle fatigues rushed them from out of nowhere. Hawke took the brunt, receiving a direct strike to the jaw which smacked his head around and knocked him off his balance.

The backpack cushioned the crash landing, but his head was still spinning from the blow to his face. He was dimly aware of several soldiers streaming into the clearing from all sides. Had they been tracking them? If so, for how long? He knew they had to be good to have pulled off such an attack. With the rest of the team engaged in hand-to-hand combat, he saw the man who had hit him, padding toward him with a bayonet in his hand.

Scrabbling in the dirt, Hawke grabbed the hem of the man's tropical combat jacket and yanked down hard, pulling him off his balance. As the guard fell sideways, Hawke sprung up off the ground and curled his hands into two tights fists. He punched the man's throat and rammed his other fist up into his lower jaw, smashing his teeth and causing him to bite through his own tongue.

His screams were muted by Hawke's hand as he pulled himself up behind his opponent and wrapped his arms around his neck and face, muffling his mouth. The man surprised him again, swinging his leg out behind him in a tight arc and hooking Hawke's legs out from under him, sending him falling backwards once again.

This time, Hawke pulled the man down with him, and the two men tumbled over the edge of the canyon. Over and over they rolled, until crashing into a bog at the bottom. Two of the soldiers called out after their friend, left the brawl and started making their way down the slope toward him.

Still wearing the cumbersome backpack, Hawke fired a jab into his opponent's face and knocked him away, then he leapt to his feet and shrugged the pack off. Beckoned the soldier forward to attack again. "C'mon, let's end this here and now."

The man lunged and they fought again. Fists swung in air full of insects as the two men waded about in the marsh, landing punches on one another, but Hawke got the last word when he hit the man in the face and sent him tottering back in the swamp. Rendered semi-conscious by the blow, he hovered in mid-air for a few seconds before falling back and striking the back of his skull on a rock.

Hawke instantly knew he was dead, and crouched down in the undergrowth, concealing himself from the other soldiers. Seeing his pack was too far away to reach, he smeared more mud on his face to further camouflage himself and scanned the area for a weapon to use. Nothing. Then he remembered what had dispatched the first soldier. He rolled the dead man over until he was face down in the marsh and hefted the blood-stained rock he had struck his skull on.

The two soldiers had made their way further down the slope now. They were peering into the dark jungle at the bottom of the canyon, trying to identify the location of the scuffling sound they had heard when Hawke and the soldier were fighting for their lives. One called out to his friend while the other fumbled for a flashlight in the pocket of his sweat-stained tactical field jacket.

Close enough to touch, Hawke leaped up and gripped the man's head and twisted it hard, breaking his neck. As the body slumped down into the marsh, the other guard's flashlight beam tracked across the ground on its way over to his position. He considered diving down behind the trunk of a nearby pink lapacho tree, but it was too far to reach in time.

He heard suppressed gunfire and saw the guard fall to his knees. He had taken a short burst of bullets from Scarlet Sloane's Sig Sauer P226. He crumpled into the marshy landscape, the switched-on flashlight falling out of the dead man's hand, hitting the shallow water with a muted thud. Then he heard his old friend's voice from higher up the slope.

"Thought you might need some help, you fat old bastard."

"Gee, *thanks*." He tossed the rock into the marsh, and without another word, he picked up his pack and climbed back up the canyon's slope until reaching Cairo at the top. When they crested the rise, the others were all aiming guns at them.

"Easy, it's just us," he said.

"What happened?" Camacho asked.

"They're dead. All of them." Looking at the bodies of the other soldiers, he didn't need to ask any questions about what had happened up here.

"Who were they?" Kamala asked.

"Zamkov's elite guard, maybe?" Nikolai said.

Hawke shook his head. "Nah, they're too young and they didn't fight hard enough. They were good trackers though."

"At least we know we're getting closer to the mesa," Ryan said.

"I'll say we are," Zeke said, pointing through a small gap in the canopy ahead of them at a scene bathed in moonlight. "Look right up there and see it for yourself."

CHAPTER NINE

Even through their night vision equipment, the mesa was unlike anything they had ever seen before. All table-top mountains were impressive, but this was in another league. Standing apart from the rest of the mountain range in eerie isolation, sheer rockfaces of sandstone and quartz rose from the surrounding rainforest like enormous manmade walls.

If it was like any other tepui, its top would be a perfectly flat plateau, but they could only guess. After a few hundred meters, the mesa disappeared into a thick blanket of tropical rainclouds. The parts of the mesa they were able to see were covered in tropical plants and steaming in the heat. It was at once the most beautiful natural thing they had witnessed and the most dangerous challenge of their lives. Waterfalls tumbled over the top of the plateau and the hoarse, raspy cry of a military macaw called out in the night.

"We're not in Kansas anymore," Ryan said.

Hawke had to agree. "And judging from the distance, I'd say that mesa is at least two thousand feet above ground level. This is going to be the climb of the year."

Kamala looked at him sideways. "For some of us, try the climb of our lives."

"Looks like that place out of *Up*," Zeke said. "I love that movie, but I never thought I'd be running around in it."

Ryan stared at the geological marvel looming above them like a monster. "The plateaus of these mountains have been totally cut off from the rest of evolution, and each one is like a perfect time capsule. Each one hosts a very distinct ecosystem. We could find literally anything up there."

"That's good to know." Lea said.

"And the bases of tepuis like these are riddled with cave systems," he continued. "Not too long ago, a team of speleologists from the University of Bologna spent nearly six weeks exploring the cave systems below Venezuela's Imawarì Yeuta. Apparently, they found over twenty kilometers of tunnels inside the mountain, and for all we know this one could be even worse."

"What the hell is a speleologist?" Scarlet said.

"They spent six weeks exploring caves," Ryan said sarcastically. "I'd give anyone else three guesses, but in your case we'd better make it five."

"I'm sorry," she said coolly. "But just how the literal fuck do you know all this stuff?"

He tapped his temple. "Eidetic memory. If you had any memory at all you'd remember that whatever I read stays in here forever… but I still say it would have made more sense to land the chopper on top of the frigging mesa."

Lea turned to him. "Sure, if you wanted to get blown out of the sky by Zamkov's surface-to-air defense system. Don't you remember what the Canadian pilot told us about that?"

"I'm just saying that's one hell of a trek."

"Which we start now," Hawke said. "Our landing position was chosen so Zamkov has no idea we're in the vicinity. Now we have a march through the jungle and then we climb the mesa. Our Canadian friend claimed the sheer faces of the mesa were guarded by Zamkov's elite forces. If so, we fight through them until we reach the top, and then we get into the compound. No one said it would be easy, mate. You're either up for it or you're not."

"I'm up for it," he said. "You don't think I'd stay down here all on my own, do you?"

"No," Scarlet said. "I don't."

"Looks like there are two ways up," Hawke said, carefully scouting the rim of the mesa. "There's a route up the face to the southeast, and another on the northeast. The rest looks fairly sheer and if there really are guards watching that part of the mountain, we'd just be sitting ducks."

"And we know from Ryan's research that the western approach is even more dangerous," Lea said.

"But we're closer to the southeast approach," Ryan whined.

"And the southeast climb is much harder," Lea said. "Wanna swap?"

"As you were."

"Right then," Hawke continued. "So we split up into two teams. Scarlet, you lead Ryan, Reaper, Jack and Lexi on the northeast route, and I'll go with Lea, Zeke, Kolya and Kamala up the southeast. Last team to the top is buying the beers when we've got Moran and this nightmare's over. Are we all clear?"

Then, they picked up their packs, checked their weapons and broke into two teams.

"Don't forget – last team to the top buys the beers," Scarlet called out through the undergrowth.

Hawke laughed. "I won't."

Then Ryan shouted, "If we survive."

Yes, Hawke thought as he looked up at the mesa, *if we survive*.

*

Empty hours passed as Hawke's team made their way through the night to the mesa. It was hard work. Moving in single file, the leader's job was to hack at the undergrowth with a machete, and the team rotated this job every quarter of an hour to give each member a rest before their next shift at the front. Drink breaks were sombre and tense. Often, no one spoke – the raging of the insects filling the sweaty night was more than enough company.

Well after midnight, they broke through a thick barrier of vegetation and found themselves in a flatter, clearer area of wetland. Trees grew in more isolated clumps, and for the first time they were able to see to the mesa properly, and the full horror of the climb that awaited them. Eerily, the lights of Zamkov's Vyraj compound produced a faint white glow above the tepui, making the stars above it paler and harder to see.

"That's one hell of place to put a secret base," Zeke said.

Kamala was staring at the vertical rockfaces, glowing silver in the Amazonian moonlight. "I never saw anything like it in my entire life. It's beautiful."

"It's dangerous," Hawke said. "We already know Zamkov has men patrolling the jungle around the mesa. The closer we get to it, the more resistance we're going to come up against."

"It's still beautiful." Her words trailed away into the night. "Nothing like that where I'm from, that's for damn sure."

"Its beauty is majestic," Nikolai said. "It reminds me of some of the Greek monasteries, built up on the rock stacks in the Pindus Mountains, or the one where we first met."

Lea recalled the battle in the Oracle's inner sanctum on Meteora. "It does look a bit like that, except…what the freaking fuck was that?"

Hawke flicked his head to her. "What?"

Lea rubbed her eyes and passed a trembling hand over her forehead. "I thought I saw something… something running through the trees over there."

"What was it?" Zeke said. "Another soldier?"

Hawke looked at his fiancée. She looked like she had seen a ghost. "Lea, what's the matter?"

She shook her head slowly and took a step back, away from the trees. "It… it was some sort of *monster*, Joe."

As Hawke scanned the trees with his monocular, Nikolai's eyes widened. "Monster?"

"It had horns, and eyes of fire and…"

"I don't know what you saw," Hawke said flatly, "but whatever it was, it's not there now."

"I didn't imagine it!"

"I'm not saying you did."

"It looked like—"

"Wait!" Hawke raised his hand to stop the conversation and drew a combat knife from his belt. "I hear something."

Lea pointed to a line of mangroves on the far side of the clearing. "Over there! Something's moving, Joe."

Zeke reached for his gun. "Must be more of Zamkov's soldiers."

"No, wait," Hawke. "It's not – hold your fire."

"Then who the hell is it?" Zeke asked.

"We're about to find out," Lea said. "Whoever it is, they're breaking through the mangroves and heading right for us."

*

Scarlet's team made slow progress, and with each step, the night seemed to get heavier and darker. After an hour, they reached a narrow river and decided to sit on the bank.

The march had been unforgiving, and they all needed food, water and some time to rest.

"This is a tough one," Ryan said.

"Sure is." Camacho bit the end off of a chocolate bar and started chewing. "And it's only just begun."

"It's the humidity," Lexi said. "And if you think marching in it is bad, wait until the fighting starts."

Reaper finished his food, drank some water and lit up one of his rolled-up cigarettes. It was narrow and crimpled and bent over in the middle, but he seemed to enjoy it well enough. He took a long drag and then perched it on his lip as he pulled out his phone and snapped a selfie. Looking at the team apologetically, he said, "One for my boys. It's not every day you find yourself in the heart of the Amazon, non?"

"Must be pretty good to have kids," Camacho said wistfully. "Someone to make everything worth it." He turned his eyes to Scarlet and slipped an arm over her shoulder.

"Forget about it, Jackie boy," she said. "I'm not exactly mother material."

He shrugged, but kept his arm where it was. "Can't blame a guy for trying."

Scarlet rummaged in her pack and found her own cigarettes, but before she could pull one from the pack, she stopped in her tracks and cocked her head. "What was that?"

"What?" Lexi asked. "You hear something?"

"A buzzing sound."

"Probably just the river," Ryan said. "Can I cadge one of those ciggies?"

"Buy your own, you cheap bast— there it is again."

Reaper nodded and looked into the sky above the trees behind them. "It's not the river."

Then, Scarlet's mouth opened in shock as she pointed into the trees and scrambled to her feet.

"Look out!" she yelled, pointing. "Incoming!"

They reacted fast, getting on their feet and turning to face what she had seen.

Ryan stared up into the darkness and saw a terrifying vision as a military-grade quadcopter drone hovered below the canopy. It was scanning the area, almost certainly using infrared optics as it searched for them. Small, compact and yet able to support and carry a light machinegun, it was a formidable weapon.

And then it found him.

Turning in his direction, the last thing he registered was a bright, white hot muzzle flash and the terrible metallic clanking sound as it opened fire on him.

CHAPTER TEN

Miles to the south, Hawke and the rest of the team watched as a solitary man ducked his head and stepped out of the last line of mangroves. In the silvery light of the moon, he saw the man was a member of one of the local tribes. He was mostly naked, except for a red loincloth, and his body was covered in paint.

They watched as the strange figure walked toward them without fear. When he got closer, Hawke saw he was wearing beads around his neck and armlets around both his upper arms. Closer still, and the man's walk was still slow, deliberate and without fear. Bright red feathers protruded from the armlets, and turquoise cotinga feathers hung from his ears.

Now he was walking right up to them. What had looked like black paint on his body was in fact red, probably mixed from crushed annatto seeds and ash, but the mask painted over his face was a strong black dye, made from genipap fruit.

"Quem é você?"

The accent was heavy but they had all heard him correctly; he was speaking Portuguese.

Hawke spoke first, in slow Spanish. It wasn't the same language, but it was close and it was all he knew. Laying down his knife in the marsh, he raised his hands to show the man his empty palms in the universal gesture of peace.

"Somos amigos."

We are friends.

The man nodded. From deep inside the black-painted face mask, they watched his eyes as they crawled all over the intruders. After more silence, he said, "Por quê você está aqui?"

Portuguese was harder to understand than Spanish, and the man's accent didn't make things any easier, but Hawke caught the last word and guessed what he had asked.

"Debemos ir…" he searched for the words and pointed to the mesa. "Debemos ir allí. Debemos ir a la mesa. We must to go to the mesa. Esta noche."

The man reacted to Hawke's use of English. "You are not Brazilians?"

Hawke's shock at hearing the man speak in his own language was tempered with a wave of relief. "No, we're not Brazilians. How do you know English?"

"An American journalist came with a missionary. They lived with us for many months. Why do you want to go up there?"

"To save our friends," Lea said.

The man was silent for a long time. Then he beckoned for them to join him. "Come with me, and we can talk."

After a quick glance at one another, Lea shrugged her shoulders. "What have we got to lose?"

"And he's walking in the direction of the mesa," Kamala said. "So we're not going back on ourselves if we follow him."

Hawke nodded. "Let's go then."

Walking in respectful silence, they crossed another stretch of tidal wetlands and salt marshes and passed through more mangroves. Weaving their way through the maze of plants and negotiating the winding, tangled root systems, they emerged to find themselves in a dense section of the jungle. Here, the man led them along a path already cut into the vegetation. It sloped downwards, and when they reached the bottom, they saw others from the tribe and the flickering of a fire through the trees.

The man turned. "We can talk here. These are my people. I am their shaman."

Felled logs surrounded a small fire, and as the shaman invited them to sit, Lea felt the eyes of dozens of tribe members all over her.

"Please, you look very strange to them. There are more isolated tribes, but we have had very limited interaction. Some missionaries, the journalist I talked about, and…" he turned two sad eyes in the direction of the mesa, "and the men on the tepui."

"You've met them?" Lea said.

"We see them fly on and off the mesa, like gods," he said with disgust. "They came here years ago and stole our lands. Many other tribes lost their lands a long time ago, to illegal logging and mining and farming. We thought we had escaped until *they* arrived."

"We want to make them leave this place," Lea said. "If we can. We have weapons."

He nodded and stared into the fire. When the shaman finally responded, he was quiet and completely unfazed by the revelation about their weapons. "We believe this place is a sacred location, one endowed by the gods with unimaginable spiritual energy. In the steam made by the river on the mesa, we are able to send messages directly to the divine creators."

"Steam?" Lea asked.

"The river boils," the shaman said.

As the old man spoke, Hawke's eyes drifted upwards into the sky, a giant vault of stars scattered across the black jungle night. He saw a satellite passing through the center of the southern cross. It glided silently with its unknown payload through the night sky. Hundreds of miles below, he returned his gaze to the shaman sitting opposite him, his face flickering amber in the campfire.

"We respect your land and your traditions," he said flatly. "We're not like the men in the compound."

The shaman nodded gently as he contemplated the foreigner's words. For once, Hawke was glad Ryan wasn't here to explain everything with logic. The last thing the shaman wanted to hear was his river explained away by scientific theories of magmatic systems and geothermal volcanic anomalies. This place, and the mesa, were sacred to these people, and that was how Hawke wanted it to stay.

The shaman nodded to himself. "Yes, to us, the mesa is a sacred place," he began sadly. "It is a home to our most important guiding spirits. We want those men to go, to leave us alone on our lands but they have a dark magic working for them."

"What do you mean?" Lea asked.

"The spirits walk here in the night," he said. "I have seen them. Others have seen them."

Lea looked across at Hawke. "What do you mean?" she asked.

The shaman's frown grew deeper. "I'm talking about jungle spirits."

Back in the day, she and Ryan had often crashed out in the evening and watched TV together, usually Discovery Channel, if her first husband had anything to do with it. She remembered now a program about a shamanic community similar to this one, but it was in Peru.

Now, a tingle ran up her spin as she recalled the monster she had seen back in the swamp. Is that what the shaman was talking about? She struggled to remember the details, to find something intelligent to say back to the shaman sitting opposite her. Maybe that tribe was called the Mayantuyaca, and they worshipped a river serpent called Yacumama. Back then, safe on her sofa with her hands wrapped around a warm coffee, she never dreamed one day she would see one of these jungle spirits with her own two eyes. She debated whether to tell the shaman or not, then she decided to go with it.

"I saw one, too."

The shaman looked at her sharply. "You saw one of the jungle spirits?"

She gave a reticent nod. "Yes, I think so. Earlier tonight just before we met you. I was walking in the jungle and I saw something running through the trees. I know I sounds crazy, but it scared the hell out of me."

"What did it look like?" the shaman asked.

"It was tall – very tall. Much taller than Joe and even bigger with it. It had the body of a lizard and the head of a snake but with bull horns. Its eyes were like balls of fire. I can't get it out of my mind."

Hawke stared at her. "Why didn't you tell us it looked like that?"

She shrugged. "Felt like an idiot."

The shaman nodded and smiled revealing broken, yellowed teeth. "You are not an idiot. You saw Boitatá. He crawls through the fields and jungles at night looking for souls. You are lucky you can still see, as many who look into his eyes are blinded."

A pocket of sap in a branch on the fire exploded, making everyone jump. Hawke noticed Lea shudder, and in over thirty degrees Celsius it wasn't because she was cold. "You really think you saw something like that?"

She gave him a hurt look. "You think I'd make something like that up?"

"No, not at all." He wanted to say more, to tell her she was mistaken, that such things don't exist, but he couldn't do it without offending the shaman.

"It is not good to doubt those you love," the shaman said.

"How did you know that we…"

"I have never looked into the fiery eyes of Boitatá," he said calmly. "But I still have my eyes."

Hawke and Lea exchanged a smile, but the moment was ended by Nikolai pulling a half bottle of vodka from his pack. He took a good slug then handed it around. Slowly it made its way around the circle, settling the nerves of everyone on the team of foreign explorers.

After a long pause, the shaman spoke again. "So, you say you are our friends and that you want to help us get rid of the monsters on the tepui."

Hawke nodded. "Yes."

"Then we will help you."

"How?" Lea asked.

"Do you promise to leave this place when you have gotten rid of the men and their machines hiding up in the clouds?"

Hawke gave another solemn nod. "Of course."

"In that case, I will lead you to the mesa. You were not going on the easiest route when I found you."

Hawke caught Lea's eye and saw a twinkle of hope. Looking at the faces of the other team members, he saw they all felt the same thing. Turning to the shaman, he gave the man a smile. "Thank you."

"We leave an hour before sunrise," the shaman said. "Now, you eat and get some sleep."

CHAPTER ELEVEN

"This way!"

Ryan barely heard the words as he dived into the river to avoid the machinegun. Camacho had found somewhere to hide along the north bank of the rushing torrent, but right now the IT geek from west London was swimming as deep as he could go. Fighting the tide in a panic, bullet trails split the black water either side of him as the quadcopter continued to track his body heat.

Deciding he could get further away if he went with the tide, Ryan gave up and let the river carry him downstream beneath the threat. For a while, the bullet trails followed him, each one getting closer as the drone sharpened its aim. Then the bullets stopped.

Breaking the surface, he saw the quadcopter chasing Reaper back into the tree line. The Frenchman was using himself as a diversion to give Ryan the time he needed to get out of the water and back along the bank to Camacho and Scarlet. Lexi was in between the river and the jungle, firing on the drone from behind the cover of a jumble of boulders.

Ryan swam for the bank and crawled out of the water back up into the insect swarms and clinging humidity. The bullets had almost been worth enduring for a few moments of relief from the heat. Wiping the water from his eyes and hair, he raised a hand and silently caught Camacho's attention. The American waved back and gestured for him to hurry up and come over to where he and Scarlet were taking cover.

He crept along the river's pebbly bank, keeping his body out of sight of the drone to reduce the chance of it tracking his heat signature. *This is one hell of a night, man*, he muttered to himself. One hell of a night.

"Over here," Scarlet called out. "Jack found some sort of tunnel."

Ryan reached his friends and peered down in the black hole Camacho had discovered underneath the overhang in the south bank.

"Mmm, looks really cosy."

Boots smacked down on the rocks behind him. He spun around to see Lexi Zhang standing there, smoke drifting from the muzzle of the Glock in her right hand. "What looks cosy?"

"Fuck cosy," Scarlet said. "Where's Reap?"

"J'suis ici," growled the Frenchman as he smashed down onto the riverbank beside them. "But unfortunately, I am not alone."

The hideous buzz of the quadcopter grew louder above their heads, and then they all saw it, wheeling in the air above the river and preparing to strafe them once again.

"Looks like we're going in." Camacho turned to Scarlet. "But it's your call."

"*I'm* fucking well going in there! You can do as you like."

They rushed inside, and Scarlet slammed her back up against the tunnel wall as she hurriedly reloaded her gun. At her side, Jack Camacho was wiping blood from his forehead while Ryan, Lexi and Reaper covered the root-tangled entrance.

Outside, they saw the drone swoop towards them but then change course and fly up over the top of the riverbank, ripping bullets into the ground with a vengeance as it zipped through the sky. As the rounds raked through the jungle behind the river, a chorus of terrified howler monkeys screeched in the night. Then, slowly, the buzzing noise of the four copters receded into the night until the sound of cicadas and bulldog bats masked it completely.

Scarlet's chest was heaving up and down as she fought to slow her breathing. "And just what the actual fuck was that?"

"It's a LAW," Camacho said.

"A what?"

Seeing the graze above his eye had stopped bleeding, he continued. "A Lethal Autonomous Weapon."

"That doesn't sound like too much fun," Ryan said. "Are we talking AI, here?"

Camacho gave a nod. "We sure are."

"You can't be talking about AI robots?" Scarlet said. "I thought they were years away?"

"Wrong again," the American said. "Even back when I was in the CIA, they were a thing, and just imagine how much they've developed since then."

Reaper was leaning against the tunnel entrance, gun pointed at the ground. "Exactly what are talking about here?"

"We're talking about full-on autonomous military robots with fully independent search, engage and destroy capabilities."

"You mean no one was controlling that thing?" Lexi asked.

"Exactly, and for all we know, Zamkov Systems could be years ahead of both the Americans and the Russians."

"You're not filling me with confidence, Jack," Scarlet said.

Lexi frowned. "When Shorten was talking about Zamkov being 10G, I thought he was bullshitting us for kicks, but now I'm not so sure."

Ryan's face paled. "Holy shit, there could be dozens of them out here in the jungle… maybe hundreds of the things."

"And all hunting us," Scarlet said. "We have to warn Joe. They'll be closer to the mesa than us. It might be even worse there."

"Do it now," Camacho said. "They might have already been engaged by them, but if not, we need to give them the heads up."

She radioed the other team over the comms, but received nothing but static in response.

"That's not good," Lexi said.

"Maybe it's the tunnel…"

Ryan looked confused. "But they should still be well in range, unless…"

Scarlet finished the sentence. "Unless Zamkov has a network of jammers blocking radio comms around the mesa."

"But they worked when we tested them before we split up," Ryan said.

Reaper shook his head. "That was before the fun and games with the robot."

"He's right," Camacho said. "Our little dust-up with the flying Short Circuit out there must have triggered a defensive mechanism around the entire area."

"Which means," Scarlet said coolly, "not only are we cut off from the rest of the team, but now Zamkov knows we're here."

"He knows someone is here," Lexi said. "Not us."

"Unless his little robots have facial rec," Ryan said. "In which case he's already running the data through his system trying to ID us. Don't forget who the guest of honor up there in his little compound is either – Jackson Moran of the DIA. It's possible Faulkner already knows we're here."

Calmer now, Scarlet dusted herself off. "Listen, let's not get ahead of ourselves here. We had a brawl with an AI robot, that's it. Making the step from that to the nearest US carrier group launching an all-out war against us is a bit of a leap."

"Cairo's right," Camacho said. "We need to keep this real."

"So, the mission stays the same," Scarlet said. "We are to ascend the northwest route of the mesa and meet with Joe's team at the top. Then we regroup and plan the assault on Zamkov's compound and snatch Moran."

"It was hard enough before," Ryan said. "And now we have an army of psychopathic killer drones trying to hunt and kill us in the jungle."

"Then we'll just have to figure out a way to destroy them," Scarlet said.

Ryan looked uneasy. "Or we could just run down inside this tunnel and see where it comes out?"

The Chinese assassin shrugged. "Suits me."

Reaper peered down into the darkness. "It could be a dead end."

"Or it could lead all the way inside the tepui,' Ryan said. "As geological formations, they're notorious for their tunnels and cave systems. They're the Swiss cheese of mountains."

A volley of gunfire crackled outside the tunnel entrance and the low, deathly buzz of the AI drone grew louder once again.

"It's back," Ryan said. "I say we go with my idea and run like scaredy cats."

Lexi looked at Ryan and said, "For once, I'm voting for *his* idea."

Without another word, they sprinted along the tunnel and prayed it led inside the base of the tepui.

CHAPTER TWELVE

"Get up, Brooke."

The former president was stretched out on the wall-mounted bed in his cell with his eyes closed. Despite the guard's angry command, he stayed there, instead crossing his arms behind his head and letting out a long, relaxed sigh.

"I said, get up!"

Footsteps. Brooke opened one eye and tipped his head. Two young soldiers were standing at the side of his bed. "Did you guys plan a picnic for the three of us? Is that what this is about?"

Without any warning, the bigger of the two men punched him in the stomach with all his might. Brooke was shocked, and doubled over in pain as he strained to get the breath back into his lungs. Two big hands grabbed his shoulders and pulled him up to his feet. Brooke checked his name badge: Schuler.

The smaller man, a corporal named Poe looked at him with contempt burning in his eyes. "Maybe next time you'll do as you're told?"

"Don't count on it, asshole."

The other man went to take a swipe at Brooke, but the corporal stopped him, blocking his hand mid-air. "No, he has to speak with the Colonel. He can't do that if you beat him up."

Schuler took a step back, deferring to the senior rank of Corporal Poe, who now locked laser beam eyes on Brooke. "Put your hands out."

Brooke obeyed, and Schuler fitted a pair of handcuffs on him.

"Any bullshit and we cuff them behind your back, got it?"

"I sure do, corporal." Brooke gave the young man the sort of smile he usually reserved for the campaign trail. "Just lead the way. I can't wait to meet the base commander. He must be a great guy."

"Just move."

With a shove between his shoulder blades, Brooke stumbled out of his cell and smacked face-first into the wall on the other side of the corridor.

"Gee, did you slip, Mr President?"

Brooke didn't rise to the bait, but gave the men a smile and a wink. "Must be getting a little clumsy in my old age, *boys*."

"Shut up and get walking," said the young one. In the light, Brooke noticed his pock-marked face and reptilian eyes. He was enjoying having so much power over a man who had once been his Commander-in-Chief.

Brooke obeyed, and started walking to the end of the corridor. It was good to be out of his cell, and to be able to stretch his legs at long last, but it didn't take long for his fears for his beloved daughter Alex and her Secret Service detail to rise to the surface of his mind.

What if they were already dead? If they were, these guys had better kill him too. If they let him live, he wouldn't stop until he'd laid waste to the entire island. It broke his heart to think of anything happening to her. She was so innocent. She was so young.

She was right in front of him.

And Agent McGee.

Brandon was pushing her along the corridor ahead of them, but they were separated by a heavy internal door, and only just visible through a narrow strip of patterned safety glass running down the right-hand side. Now he saw both Brandon and his daughter had seen him, too.

Brooke thought fast, manoeuvring slightly to his right to obscure the door's window from the two soldiers behind him. They would be through the door in seconds, wheelchair and all, and then things could get dangerous. If his guards got the chance to fight back, Alex would be a sitting duck.

She would be killed.

He and Brandon caught each other's eye. They each knew what the other man was thinking, and when Brandon and Alex reached the door and kicked it open, Brooke threw himself to the floor, hands still cuffed in front of him.

The sound of the firing gun in the enclosed corridor was terrific. Brooke looked up at Alex and saw she was looking away at the wall, hands clamped over her ears as Brandon drilled a mag full of nine mil holes through the two soldiers. When Brooke heard their bodies slump down to the floor, he knew the job was done and it was safe to get up.

Alex was looking at him now, and Brandon was releasing the mag from the weapon's grip.

"Dad! You're still alive!"

Brooke leaned over and gave his daughter a tight hug. "Thank God you are, too."

Brandon smacked a new mag back inside the grip and checked the corridor was still clear. "We need to get you out of here, Mr President."

"And in a hurry," Brooke said. "We need to get as far as we can away from this place."

"I thought I saw an external fire door a few corridors back," Alex said.

Brooke gave her a smile of reassurance. "Then that's our next stop."

And then they were gone.

CHAPTER THIRTEEN

Jackson Moran had been in Vyraj for nearly twenty-four hours before being summoned by Nikita Zamkov at dawn. When he finally met the reclusive Russian technology entrepreneur, he immediately wished he hadn't. His DIA briefing had filled in most of the blanks about the strange man – the son of a senior-ranking Communist Party official, childhood in Moscow's wealthy Rublyovka district, antisocial tendencies at university – but seeing him for the first time in the flesh was something else.

In the flesh.

A poor choice of words, Moran considered, as he watched the ghostly pale Zamkov slide some raw meat into his mouth and wipe the blood from his lips.

Now I understand why they call him the Butcher...

"Mr Moran, how good of you to join me. Please allow me to welcome you to Vyraj."

As he spoke, the voice-controlled smart-home system automatically cleared the vast wall of switch-glass from an opaque to transparent and revealed a breathtaking view of the vast jungle stretching across the top of the mesa outside the compound. Beyond, an ocean of cloud tops surrounded the tepui, giving the impression they were literally on top of the world.

Moran controlled himself. No sense showing you're impressed. "Vyraj – that's a mythical place in Slavic folklore, isn't it?"

"You are well briefed, Jackson – may I call you Jackson?"

Before Moran could reply, Zamkov continued. "Vyraj is an ancient Slavic conception of paradise, but as I always say, why wait for death to experience paradise?"

Another voice-activated control brought an AI robot into the room.

When he turned, Moran was startled by what he saw. The machine wasn't exactly lifelike – the smart-skin wasn't reflecting light in the same way as the real thing, and though perfect in appearance in every way, there was something unsettlingly dead about the eyes. As it drew closer, he also noticed it was unable to walk naturally. Its progress across the ocean of polished concrete was slow and awkward.

Zamkov looked at it as a father watches a beloved child, and then turned a more critical eye to Moran. "What will you have to drink?"

"Just a still water, thanks."

"Two still waters, Yakov."

The robot turned an expressionless face away from his master and walked back out of the room. Zamkov turned beaming eyes to Moran. "I am very proud of my work here, but Yakov 2.0 is my crowning glory."

"Yakov 2.0?"

Zamkov was struggling to contain his excitement. "And Yakov 3.0 is also coming along well. We're having some problems but the AI inside 3.0 is explaining to me how to improve it. It's much smarter than I am."

"But he's not ready for the world yet?"

Zamkov's smile faded. "I think perhaps the world is not ready for him."

Moran turned and watched the machine leave the room, its footsteps receding away down the hall. "It's very impressive."

"He," Zamkov corrected him, a wild flash in his eyes. "He is very impressive."

"Of course," Moran said, backtracking fast. "He is very impressive."

This guy is straight up-and-down crazy as a box of frogs.

Zamkov stared at him for a moment and then turned to face the window. Moran wondered what was going through his mind, but he knew what was going through his own. His orders had come right from the top of the DIA and they were simple – secure a defense contract with Zamkov Systems to supply their proprietary AI autonomous weapons to the US military. The deal would be highly lucrative for Zamkov, but was Top Secret. No one could ever know where Faulkner was shopping for killer robots.

Moran decided to placate the strange Russian after his earlier faux pas. "This is quite a place you have here."

"I built Vyraj as a testament to the power of my genius."

And modest, too…

"Well, it's an incredible site."

"It gives me what I need to work, Jackson. Total privacy and isolation, plus limitless room to test my products."

Talking of which…

Moran heard the same creepy footsteps and turned to see Yakov walking back into the enormous room. He was carrying a silver tray holding two glasses of still, chilled water. When he reached them, his artificial mouth bent into a warped smile. "Your water, sir."

Zamkov looked at Moran, encouraging him with a silent nod of his head.

The American took the hint and lifted a glass of water from the tray. Zamkov did the same and took a long sip. "Thank you, Yakov."

Moran sipped his water and smacked his lips. "Just what I needed. The dehumidifiers in this place really dry you out."

Zamkov glared at him. "Well?"

"I'm sorry?"

"Aren't you going to thank Yakov for bringing you your water?"

"He's just a—."

Zamkov's eyes narrowed. "He's just a what?"

"I'm sorry," Moran said quickly. Feeling foolish, he turned to the robot. "Thank you for my water, Yakov."

"You are welcome."

Zamkov gave a crooked smirk and dismissed Yakov. As the machine hobbled back out of the room, Moran watched every step. He'd seen videos of AI robots on YouTube. They were impressive and he knew the US military had covert programs that were even more advanced, but this was further ahead than anything he had seen before. Not much longer and there would be no way to tell the difference between an AI robot and a person, unless you cut them open. Even the fake skin would be warmed to body temperature.

Despite the potential this technology had for military purposes, he couldn't help but think the whole thing was downright creepy. Worse, being forced to thank the robot was humiliating. He wondered if in a few years, he'd have to thank his toaster for making breakfast, and then took another sip of his water.

"It will not be long, Jackson, before AI rules this entire planet, but enough about technology – tell me," he said without pausing, "have you met Valentina?"

"Valentina?"

"She's my fiancée. We're to get married very soon. It's all good and well, being surrounded by robots and all this technology, but a man needs a real companion, don't you think?"

Moran was unsure how to answer. "Yes, I guess so."

"She loves what I am doing here even more than I do. You are married, I understand."

"Yes, we have two kids."

"Two daughters?"

Moran bristled slightly. It seemed Zamkov was as well briefed about him as he was about the Russian.

"What's the matter? You thought I'd have you to stay here in my inner sanctum without learning everything about you? If you do, then you disappoint me."

"You do whatever you have to, Mr Zamkov. I'm just here as a representative for the US Government."

"Quite, quite…"

A long, difficult silence stretched out, and Moran blinked first.

"Perhaps I'll meet Valentina later."

"Perhaps, but she is very busy in the labs. She's been working very hard for me here for a long time and I plan to reward her with the greatest prize a man can give a woman."

"What's that?"

"*That*," he said, slowing his words, "is personal – between my fiancée and me." Another of those chilling grins. "I'm sure you understand."

"Of course."

A smile, of sorts, returned to Zamkov's face. "Now, you must let me tell you all about my grandfather."

"Your grandfather? My briefing said you had no living family."

Zamkov laughed. "You're going to love hearing all about it."

*

Across the compound in Sector 7M, a young man in a white lab coat was testing the viability of a new batch of printed circuit boards. It was important work, and Mr Zamkov had been very clear about his department meeting the deadline for getting it done. Taking a break, he looked up from the bench and watched the dawn light over the jungle canopy as it swayed in the breeze beyond the compound.

Then he heard the door open, and hurried back to work.

"Progress report," said a woman's voice.

He turned and saw Valentina Kiriyenko standing behind him. The way the low sun streamed in through the venetian blinds and brushed her cheekbones made her look more beautiful than ever, but he knew how dangerous she was. Everyone knew. She was too close to Zamkov to be trusted.

"Ninety percent done," he said.

She looked at the clock on the wall. "But the deadline is in less than an hour, Grigori."

He felt suddenly warm and ran a finger around his collar. "The work will be done very soon after Mr Zamkov's deadline. There is no need to worry."

She frowned. "Very soon after the deadline is not by the deadline."

"No, but it's important work, and it must be done carefully if—"

She turned on her heel and walked to the door. "I'll have to report this to Niki."

"No, please! There's no need."

"A deadline is a deadline," she said, now speaking in neat, clipped Russian. "You have failed the project."

He called out to her, but she closed the door. When he heard the lock turn, he knew he was in trouble. He had heard rumors about what happened to workers who failed

Zamkov, and he wanted none of it. Working fast but methodically, he started checking the rest of the windows and doors in the lab. Somehow, he had to get out of this place before Valentina reported back to the Butcher.

CHAPTER FOURTEEN

A third of the way up the mesa, the shaman stared up into the clouds and told them it was time for him to return to his people. He had kept his word and led them through a maze of floodplain forests and rainforest slopes covered in tangles of vines, bromeliads and towering palms. Hawke soon realized they were going in a very different route to the one he had planned out, and when they arrived at the mesa, he estimated the shaman had shaved hours off their journey.

He wished them luck and wandered back off down to the foot of the mesa, while the rest of them ascended several hundred feet before taking a break and sipping some water. On the eastern horizon, the first signs of dawn showed themselves in a pale rainbow streak of pinks and oranges low in the sky. Ahead of them, the track was narrow and rocky, almost made into a tunnel by the dense foliage growing at its side.

Hawke rummaged around in his pack and pulled out some food. Sharing it around, he looked overhead and saw the mesa wall disappearing into the clouds.

"Not much longer before the real climbing begins."

They all knew what that meant. Hawke had climbed El Capitan in California, so he knew what he was doing. Others on the team had some basic experience of rock-climbing, including some on sheer rockfaces, but this was something else. Mercifully, their new proximity to the mesa had allowed them to see the face wasn't as sheer as they had believed from further away in the jungle; small ledges and fissures criss-crossed the ascent and offered them a fighting chance.

Hawke pushed back against a broken boulder and closed his eyes. The strong scent of damp soil, decaying vegetation and plants covered in moisture reminded him of his days training in Belize. Beside them, a line of leaf-cutter ants marched across the track and vanished back into the shaded gloom of the undergrowth.

Kamala screwed the top back on her water bottle and slid it into her pack. "This place is magical. Why the hell did I never visit before this?"

"Smells like a garden center," Lea said.

Hawke said nothing, but couldn't hide the smile on his lips. Yes, it did smell like a garden center. That was why he loved the jungle.

The never-ending buzz of insects roared all around them, but the hum of the cicadas was fading away now the sun's light was breaking over the ancient landscape. A bird called high above them, swooping out of the cloud ceiling and disappearing back up inside it. Below, a blue morpho butterfly flitted out of the thicket and danced around them before flying away down the track.

Zeke belched loudly as he screwed the cap back on his water and slapped at a mosquito on his upper arm. Crushing the insect in the middle of his 7th Cavalry Regiment tattoo, its mangled body fell down onto the rocky ground. "I hate the jungle."

"Me too," Nikolai said.

"Damn straight," said Zeke. "Nowhere to drive a tank in a place like this, that's for sure."

Hawke checked the altimeter on his watch. "We're probably halfway up," he said. "We'd better get going."

Lea got up, slipped on her pack and headed up the track first. In the lead now, she had only made a few steps when she saw something moving up ahead. Her heart skipped a beat as she realized it was the same monster she had seen before, down on the plains.

"Get down!" she called out.

Everyone on the team immediately ducked and reached for their weapons. Hawke peered up the track to the front. "What is it?"

"I… I don't know." Her voice was weak and uncertain. She crouched low in the foliage, blinking her disbelieving eyes in the early dawn twilight. No, it was still there, stalking through the jungle at incredible speed. It was a snake. It was a lizard. Grotesque bull's horns twisted out of the sides of its head. And the eyes… eyes of burning fire.

Just as the shaman had described.

For a moment, words failed her. Hiding in the thicket with bated breath and her heart pounding with fear, she could not bring herself to believe what she was seeing. She wanted to call out to Hawke or one of the others, but it would give away her position. She felt the panic rise inside her, and worked hard to fight it back down.

You're just hallucinating.

Yes, that was it. She must have somehow ingested a hallucinogenic substance from something in the jungle. She'd read somewhere you could start tripping just by touching LSD – maybe she'd brushed her skin up against something even more powerful growing right here in this rainforest.

The hideous monster raced along the path, twisting its head from side to side as it scanned the trees for any sign of life. She crouched lower, almost curling into a ball. With the gun gripped her in hand, she watched as it moved out of sight, running along the track and slipping out of sight in the undergrowth.

She made her way back down the track, terrified by what she had seen. "It's the thing I saw earlier, Joe. It's up there ahead of us, somewhere."

He gripped his gun. "We have to use this track. There's no other way."

With his words hanging in the air, Kamala called out from behind them. She was the last in line, fifty feet lower on the track and she was staring through the foliage at the sky. "Are those birds?"

Nikolai was first to get to her. "I don't think so."

Hawke and Lea walked back down to the others. "Birds?"

"Of course they're birds," Zeke said dismissively. "Just what the hell else would they be?"

"Bats, maybe?" Nikolai said.

Hawke watched the swarm draw nearer, their black shapes nothing more than silhouettes against the bright sunrise behind them.

"They don't look like birds to me," he said calmly. "Too big."

Kamala shielded her eyes from the sun with her hand and studied the strange shapes. "Maybe it's a flock of some sort of crazy Amazonian vultures or something?"

Lea shook her head. "The king vulture's habitat is mostly lowland forests, but I don't think they fly in a pattern like that. Besides, it's a venue of vultures, not a flock, or a kettle if they're circling a corpse."

Kamala raised an eyebrow. "Next time I play scrabble, you're invited."

Lea laughed. "You'd be better playing with Ryan – he taught me all this stuff."

Hawke walked over to them. As his eyes focused on the approaching shapes, a massive chunk of the rockface a few yards to his left exploded in a savage burst of sandstone fragments.

"Shit, we're under attack!"

Kamala dived down to the ground. "What the fuck?"

"They're drones," Hawke called out. "And they're armed with lasers."

"I thought that meant red laser beams!" she said.

"Only in the movies," Zeke said. "In real life, directed energy weapons fire a beam invisible to the naked eye. What's blowing my mind is how they got the damn things on board a bunch of drones."

"It seems Zamkov Systems really *are* well ahead of the US," Kamala said.

The substantial quadcopter drones zipped over their heads and broke formation. Each one turning in a wide arc before heading back in the direction of the mesa rockface.

"If we don't think of something fast," Zeke said, "I'm calling it first – we're toast."

Hawke hefted his submachine gun and opened fire on the drones. Sweeping the barrel from side to side, he took out the two in the front before the others broke ranks and took evasive action.

"Turns out they're not so tough," he called out.

"But they'll be back," Lea said.

"We won't be here." Hawke slung the weapon over his shoulder and headed back up the track. "We're getting to the top of this mesa and we're doing it right now. Drones, fire-eyed monsters and anything else between me and Moran can get fucked."

Lea shrugged and looked over at Zeke. "That's one way of looking at it."

With the drones almost out of sight now, Zeke picked up his backpack and gun and joined Kamala at the rear. "Looks like we've got a hell of a day ahead of us."

CHAPTER FIFTEEN

"I see light at the end of the tunnel."

Scarlet and the rest of the team caught up with Ryan. They also saw the light, and after a night spent checking compass readings in an underground labyrinth crawling with scorpions, it was a serious relief.

Using their machetes to hack a way through thick spiderwebs and tangled root systems, they emerged into the jungle once again. Still gloomy despite the later hour, they knew why when they followed Ryan's pointing finger and looked up into the sky and saw the mesa towering above them.

"We're right at the base."

"Fuck me, we did it," Lexi said.

"And in really good time." Reaper stared up too, amazed by what he saw. "Taking this tunnel has saved us many hours of hard work hacking through the jungle. We're probably ahead of Hawke."

Scarlet gave the others a wry smile. "Now all we have to do is climb to the top."

"Three hours," Reaper said, opening his pack and pulling out his water canteen. "Then, we will be at the top and we can ask Zamkov for some lunch."

Camacho pushed out a weary laugh. "You think he's got a spare shower?"

"Oui," he grumbled. "Naturellement."

The climb was hard going. Reaper's estimate wasn't far off, and after four hours they reached the top of the winding track. In places, they'd had to use ropes and alpine hammers to shift up a level when a track ran out or was blocked with rockfall. Now, they slumped down on the edge of the mesa and stared out across the floodplains and rainforests as they drank more water.

Ryan tipped his canteen upside down and not a single drop came out. “That’s the last of the water.”

“There’s no shortage of fresh water here,” Reaper said. “We can boil it to make it safe.”

Flit… flit, flit-flit-flit.

Ryan spun around, staring at the others with confused eyes. “What the fuck?”

“Bullets!” Scarlet had heard too many bullets tracing past her head not to know instantly what was happening. “We’re under fire. Take cover!”

They rolled away from each other, Reaper and Lexi in one direction, Scarlet, Camacho and Ryan in the other.

“Split up!” Scarlet called out.

“What, now?” Ryan asked.

“Now,” was the response. “Right now.”

Reaper and Lexi rolled down a slope leading away from the edge of the mesa, just south of their original position. The Frenchman’s cut and bruised head was spinning by the time he reached the bottom of the slope. He saw Lexi come to a stop a few meters to his north, but there was no sign of the others.

The Chinese assassin sat up and cocked her head. “It’s stopped. The firing’s stopped.”

He nodded. “Oui – but I hear something else. Boots. Soldiers.”

She leapt to her feet and reached for her gun, but it was gone. “Damn it.” She looked up the slope. “Must have lost it on the way down. You?”

“Same thing.”

Then the firing resumed.

“Where are they?”

“Over there,” he said. “We go this way, non?”

They hacked their way through vines and giant tropical pitcher plants. Each step of the way, the soldiers behind them were closing the gap, then Reaper stumbled down an embankment, reaching out whenever a branch offered something to steady himself with. Lexi slipped through the foliage and found him searching for something.

"What are you looking for?"

"There are more soldiers ahead of us," he said. "I heard them running. Their boots were crunching on gravel. There must be a path."

"Then we must be getting closer to the compound," she said.

"Oui."

Desperately straining his eyes in the jungle half-light in search of the path, he was suddenly aware of the sound of the enemy as their boots crunched on the broken branches behind him. Tearing at the foliage with his bare hands, he heard Lexi cursing at his side as she joined the search.

"When those guys get here, we have one hell of a fight on our hands, Reap."

He wiped the sweat from his forehead and hurriedly adjusted his bandana. "Tell me something I don't know."

"There!" she said. "See it?"

Reaper breathed a sigh of relief. For a while he'd started to wonder if the blast had knocked them too far down the slope and they'd never find the path. Seeing the track cut into the thick foliage gave him a shot of hope. Taking hold of Lexi by her slim, muscular shoulders he spun her around until they were face to face. "I could kiss you, mon ami!"

Lexi raised an eyebrow. "Maybe later, Vincent."

A bullet flew between their faces, ripped through a rain-soaked banana leaf and buried itself in the trunk behind it, showering them in flying shreds of bark.

"Holy shit!" she said.

As they scrambled down to the path, the Frenchman turned to her. "And it's Reaper – I'm…"

"I know, I know," she said. "You're on a mission!"

"Merci bien."

They sprinted down the narrow path, ducking and dodging thick undergrowth where it had grown back over the cutaway. Behind them, they heard the report of distant submachine guns echoing sharply through the jungle.

Another round whistled past Lexi's head, missing her by millimetres. She cried out but never stopped running.

Reaper's heavy frame was built for fighting and long-term stamina, not fast sprints, and now he was starting to fall back behind the Chinese assassin. With every thundering footstep he took, he thought about his twins back at home in France. Louis and Leo, probably playing in the safety of their Provence villa at this very moment, blissfully unaware of the terrible danger their father was in.

"Maybe time to end this madness," he panted.

"Keep running, Reaper!"

"I'm on it," he called back. "All over it like a boss."

But he was slowing down, unlike the soldiers behind him.

Lexi glanced over her shoulder as she sprinted. Seeing his pace slow, she ran back over to him. "Maybe we should hide?"

"Never!" he said. "You go on and I'll make a stand here and fight them. Slow them down and give you chance to get up to the compound."

"Desert a fellow member of ECHO?" She looked almost offended. "What do you think I'm made of?"

He gave his classic Gallic shrug. "Then we fight!"

"And here they are!" she said.

When the mighty legionnaire smashed the first soldier, he went down like a safe falling off the back of a truck and hit the ground hard and heavy. Cracking his head on the gravel path he passed out seconds later, giving Lexi the opportunity to wedge her boot under his midriff and kick him over the side of the path. As he rolled down in the foliage at the side of the track, she dusted her hands off and turned to face her old friend. "One down, Reap!"

"You make it sound almost boring."

The second soldier was a tougher nut to crack, pulling back his rifle and pile-driving the weapon's heavy metal stock into Reaper's face. Or at least that was the plan.

Reaper saw it coming and sidestepped the attack, giving himself just enough time to ram a meaty fist up into the man's ribcage. They all heard the crack and then the soldier let out a pained grunt as the pain from his broken rib radiated up through his body.

"You should have stayed in bed today, mon ami."

Lexi weighed up the words. "True story," she said. "Never a good idea to chase the Reaper here around the jungle."

Still in agony from the broken bone, he doubled over and took a step away from them as he tried to get his breath back. He reached down into an ankle holster and pulled out a six-inch combat knife. The sharp steel teeth of its serrated edge glinted in the soft glow of the equatorial sun, filtered by the thick canopy, but Reaper was unfazed.

"Is this supposed to impress me?"

The man said nothing but repressed the pain of his broken rib and lunged forward, slashing the knife in their faces. Alone now, he was showing no sign of fear, and when he lunged at them, it was with the conviction of a killer.

The blade was aimed at the Frenchman, but Reaper sidestepped as Lexi pivoted on her leg and brought her right boot up into the man's face. His head snapped back and for a moment he stood still and silent, arms hanging at his sides and vacant eyes staring into the middle distance.

Lexi approached him and gently touched him in the chest, sending him crashing back into the foliage and tumbling down the slope. "Easy as cherry pie, mon brave." She turned to Reaper and expected to see his battered workbench of a face impressed by her use of his mother tongue. Instead he was nowhere to be seen.

"Reap?"

"Over here."

She followed the gruff French accent off the other side of the path and into the rainforest. She saw him standing in front of a twelve-foot high fence, topped with razor wire.

"The compound?" she said.

"The compound. We're going to need my pack. It has pliers. If we go back up to find it, and our weapons, we can look for Cairo, Jack and Ryan. Then, we go through this fence and go meet Mr Zamkov… enfin."

She grinned at him. Her slim face was suddenly full of wicked intent as they high-fived. "At last."

CHAPTER SIXTEEN

Halfway up the slope they ran into Scarlet, Camacho and Ryan, who had Reaper's pack over his right shoulder. The five of them had no luck finding Lexi's pack or either of their weapons. Lost to the jungle forever, they left them behind and marched back down to the fence.

"Cutting this thing's gonna trigger the defense system," Ryan said. "We're all cool with that, right?"

"We're not *cool* with it," Scarlet said. "But what other choice do we have? We haven't got time to follow the buggering thing all around the perimeter in the hope Zamkov forgot to secure part of the compound. We're going in, here and now."

Ryan narrowed his eyes. "I *love* it when you talk dirty."

Reaper shook his head, slipped the eight inch pliers from the bag and crawled on his belly through the marshy wetland until he was at the base of the fence. The high-tensile fencing wire twanged noisily in the jungle gloom as he cut through it.

"Right, everyone through. Vite!"

Chances were good that Ryan was right, and that right now up in the compound an alarm was sounding. Everyone got that, and hurried through the hole as fast as they could. On the other side of the fence now, they continued to follow the downward slope until they reached the edge of a colossal ravine. Pulling up to a stop, but keeping low in the foliage for cover, they studied the new landmark and followed the course of a silver slice of river twisting along the bottom of the ravine.

"Is that smoke?" Lexi said.

"No," Ryan said. "It's steam. There a river in Peru somewhere. It's so hot, it's almost at boiling point. This must be a similar thing."

"In that case," Camacho said. "I'm glad I forgot my swim trunks."

"Shame." Scarlet raised an eyebrow and looked the American up and down. "You look good in those."

"Why, thank you, babe."

Lexi glared at the Englishwoman. "Maybe if you got your mind out of his trunks, we might make better progress right now?"

"Oh, yeah?"

"Yeah!" Lexi said, taking a step over to where Scarlet was standing with Camacho. "Because if there's one thing that—"

And then she was gone.

Tumbling through an unknown darkness and with no way to stop herself. Gathering her thoughts, she worked out which way was up and spun around in the air like a high-diver, head at the top and feet pointing straight down. It was a smart thing to do, because a lake of black water was racing up to meet her. She pinched her nose and ripped through the surface. If she had landed any other way, she knew she would be dead.

She swam to the surface, breathing out in controlled bursts as she powered herself up out of the cold, black water. Reaching the top, she burst out into the low light of a cave and gasped for breath. Still dazed from the fall, she stared up at the hole she had fallen through at least a hundred feet above her and couldn't believe she had survived the fall.

She slowed her breathing now, flicked her hair away from her face and scanned the surface of the cave pool for her friends. Closest was Reaper, treading water as he joined her in the search for the others.

Scarlet was next to reach the surface, crashing hard into reality with a desperate gasp. "Holy fucking shit, that's cold!"

"We can't find Ryan," Lexi called out.

"I'm up here!"

She manoeuvred in the water so she could tip her head back and look up. When her eyes adjusted to the daylight streaming in through the hole high above her, she saw him now. He was hanging upside down with his ankle snagged in the tangled root system of one of the trees. Some of the roots of another tree a few meters to his right stretched all the way down into the surface of the water.

"Are you okay?" she called up.

"I've been better," he said weakly. "I'd make a joke about hanging around, but I think I just lost my sense of humor."

"Thank heaven for small mercies," Scarlet said.

Ryan craned his neck, studying his predicament. "How the hell am I going to get down?"

Lexi judged the distance between him and the network of roots reaching down to the cave pool. "If you can untangle your foot, you could jump to those roots and climb down."

Above, they all heard the rasping buzz of another drone.

Ryan's bag was hanging under his head. He pulled it up and reached inside for a knife. "If that fucker comes in here, I'm a dead man."

"Then stop pratting about and free your ankle," Scarlet said.

Reaper started swimming for the shore. "We should get out of the water. We can walk around the pool and get closer to the roots from the other side."

When they reached the other shore, Ryan had made it down the roots and was dusting himself off.

A shovel hand gripped his shoulder. "Are you okay, mon ami?"

He nodded. "I think so."

"You think that was a booby trap?" Camacho asked.

"Maybe," Ryan said. "But it's not an uncommon feature in a place like this. There are so many caves and water holes."

"So," Lexi said coolly. "Are we fucked, or what?"

"We're not fucked," Ryan said. "It's unlikely this pool formed in isolation. There has to be a way out of here through the cave system."

Lexi peered down one of the many gaping black holes running around the outer edge of the shore. "They seem scary."

"Caves inside tepuis are pretty much the most isolated places on earth. They're totally cut off from outside influence, including biological evolution. The species found in these places are totally unique, with each tepui hosting a completely different ecosystem. Most of the flora and fauna found down here will exist nowhere else in the world."

Lexi scowled. "And how the fuck is that supposed to make it not scary?"

"It's not, but consider yourself briefed."

She raised her finger in the center of his face.

"Then we go in that one," Scarlet said, ending the moment. "It's pointing in the direction of the compound."

They made their way inside. Less than twenty meters inside the tunnel, they pulled out their Maglites and switched them on. Ryan shone his beam overhead and along the walls, and the bright light made the quartzite in the rock sparkle like diamonds all around them.

"Super speleothems," Ryan said.

Scarlet gave Camacho an apologetic look. "He means stalactites. That's how Ryan says stalactites."

"And stalagmites." He shone his torch along the roof of the cave. "That's why I said speleothems. It's easier than saying stalactites and stalagmites."

She lowered her voice. "Hard to believe he was married to Lea once. Fuck knows what they had in common."

"Now, now," Camacho said. "Be nice."

They followed the cave system for another hour, gradually making their way back up to the surface. The jungle on top of the mesa was even thicker and more impenetrable than down on the wetlands, and as Ryan had predicted, full of strange new plants none of them had ever seen before, but what got their attention was the bright, flashing reflection of the sun on a large, white spherical building far to the south, in the center of the tepui.

"It's the compound," Reaper said. "We made it."

Scarlet was sceptical. "Not yet, we didn't. You hear that?"

"Not another fucking drone?" Ryan asked.

"No. Something on foot – it's heading right for us."

"Man, this place is just full of surprises," Camacho said.

They dived for cover as the bullets started to fly, but for one of them, it was too late.

CHAPTER SEVENTEEN

Fear pumped through Alex like high-octane gasoline. On the run now, she looked up to her father and felt another wave of relief. He might be covered in cuts and bruises, but her father was alive, and so was Brandon. Now, as the Secret Service agent pushed her down yet another corridor, Jack Brooke was covering them all with one of the dead and disarmed soldiers' compact machine pistols.

"Are we just going around in circles?" she cried out.

"No," Brandon said. "We're heading west whenever we can. I figure this place has to run out sooner or later. Eventually, we have to hit an outside wall, right?"

"Sure, if you say so."

"Sure I do," Brandon said. "Look – it's a fire escape and it's leading away in a westerly direction. We'll go through here and…"

Alex screamed. "Brandon… look out!"

Soldiers burst out of the doors, armed to the teeth with automatic weapons. An older sergeant in the front and two younger men behind him. "Lay down your guns and put your hands up!"

Brandon didn't hesitate. He stepped in front of Alex and Brooke, putting his body between theirs and the threat as he drew his gun.

Behind him, Brooke brought his gun up into the aim, firing in controlled bursts on the soldiers. The younger man at the back retreated behind the cover of the metal doorway, but the older sergeant in the lead was cut down in a second.

"Mr President, you have to get your daughter out of here!"

"I'm not leaving you behind, Agent McGee!"

"We have no cover, sir! Head for the last door behind us on the right. I'll keep these guys busy here."

The other soldiers swung back around the doorway and unleashed a rapid and sustained attack on Brandon, making sure not to hit Brooke or Alex. The young Secret Service agent emptied his magazine on the soldiers, taking one of them out, but the last man standing got the last shot, blowing a hole right through Brandon's chest and felling him like a redwood.

Alex screamed.

Brooke raked the soldier with rounds until his smoking corpse crashed down in the blood-splattered fire escape. Sprinting over to Brandon, he knew before he slid to a halt beside him that he had no chance of surviving.

"Hang in there, buddy," he said, ripping open his shirt and looking at the gunshot wound. He looked up Alex and saw tears streaming down her face.

"Brandon!" she said.

"I'm just shit out of luck, Alex…" his voice grew weaker. "You have to go with your Dad now. You have to stay safe, both of—

"Brandon?"

No response, and then his head rolled over to the side. Dead, vacant eyes.

"Oh, my *God!*"

Brooke was firing on a new wave of soldiers. "We have to go, honey!"

"Where?"

Turning away from their dead friend, they saw Colonel Blanchard stepping over the cooling corpses of his soldiers. He was flanked by half a dozen more men, and he didn't look very happy.

Walking over to Brooke, he grabbed him by the collar and heaved him to his feet. “You killed some of my best men, Jack.”

“Why don’t you give me a gun and see how many more I can kill?”

Blanchard’s lip curled. “Because, you son of a *bitch*, they’d shoot back and take you out of the game here and now.” He lowered his voice. “And I can’t let that happen. You see, President Faulkner has something a hell of a lot more fun planned for you and your little girl.”

“You leave Alex out of this, you bastard!”

Blanchard released his prisoner and pushed him back over to Alex. Taking a step back to the soldiers standing behind him, he pointed down at Brandon. “Get this place cleaned up, and take them back to their cells… no, wait – get them in to solitary. See how that cools their jets.”

*

The man called himself only by his last name: Machete. No one knew his first name. So much time had passed since he had last used it, sometimes he forgot it, too. Stalking through his beloved jungle with a seventeen inch bayonet in his hand, he considered when might be the last time he really had used his name.

When he signed the papers to leave C Op Esp, the Brazilian Special Operations Command?

Yes, sir – that must be it.

Ten years in the Comando de Operações Especiais had left a deep mark on Machete’s soul, especially some of the domestic antiterror operations. His mind summoned a memory of submachine guns growling in the dark during a room clearance at a compound in Cracolândia, but that was a long time ago. He was not a young man anymore, and Mr Zamkov was a demanding employer. If the security chief had told him intruders had invaded the tepui, then it was his job to neutralize the threat.

And he was doing just that. Seconds ago, he had definitely hit one of the enemy as they had tried to dive for cover. An older man, with silver hair. Well-built. Maybe ex-military, but it didn't matter. Whoever he was, he was with two slim, athletic-looking women – one maybe American or English and one Chinese. There were others, too – a man that looked like he might be half-grizzly bear and another younger man.

It didn't matter.

They would all die here today on this mesa.

CHAPTER EIGHTEEN

Hawke's team reached the top of the mesa and found themselves confronted not with more jungle, as they had expected, but with an enormous canyon. Resting and sipping some water, they studied its geology and worked out where it was in relation to the compound.

According to Ryan's earlier briefing, it was standard terrain for the plateau at the top of a tepui. At the bottom of the ravine, a river swollen with rain from the recent monsoon trough snaked away into the dense jungle. Nowhere seemed to offer a good place to traverse the canyon, not without trekking several miles in either direction.

And then he looked closer.

"Is that water steaming?"

Kamala stood beside him, wiping her forehead with the back of her arm. "Huh?"

"Steam," he repeated. "It looks like the river is steaming."

"Oh, I see it now." She furrowed her brow. "It *does* look like steam."

Lea and Nikolai traipsed up the bank to the edge of the canyon. Behind them, Zeke took a moment to have a long drink, and then joined his friends.

"Yeah, that's steam all right," the Texan said. "You guys never hear of the Boiling River?"

Four blank faces.

"You never even heard of it?"

Kamala made a face. "You seem genuinely disappointed."

"It's a legend, man! Like the Lost City of the Incas."

"That's not a legend," Lea said. "But carry on."

He caught a twinkle in her eyes when she spoke of the Lost City, but ignored it. "I read all about it in the National Geographic back on base years ago. The Boiling River is located deep inside the Peruvian part of the Amazon and it takes hours to get there in four-wheel drive trucks."

"Nearly as remote as here then," Nikolai grizzled.

"So anyways, the river starts off cold but gradually heats up until it reaches just under boiling point. Heated by underground springs. The water isn't exactly hot enough to turn into a rolling boil but anything that falls in it is D-E-A-D dead."

"But this is not Peru, Zeke," Kamala said.

"No, it's not," said Hawke. "But that doesn't mean it's not a boiling river. We're not that far away and whatever is going on with the springs in Peru is obviously happening here, too. I think it might be a good idea if everyone makes a point of not falling into this river."

"Not unless you want to get poached like an egg," Nikolai said.

"And that's what will happen," Zeke said. "Animals fall into the Boiling River all the time and they just boil to death."

Lea winced. "I think I've heard enough. Of all the ways to go out of this world, being boiled alive ain't one I'm looking at."

"Wait," Nikolai said, hushing the conversation. "Did anyone else hear gunfire over there?"

Kamala shook her head. "No, I don't think so."

"There it is again."

"I hear it now." Hawke twisted his body to the right and tipped his head, concentrating hard on the direction the Russian monk had indicated. "Over there, to our west. Quite far away, though – maybe half a mile or more."

"Must be Scarlet's team." Zeke delivered the words with some solid respect. "Damn it, I hope they're all right."

Nikolai's face curved down into a sad frown. "Me too. Hearing them under attack like this, it's just too bad. Maybe we should go and check it out?"

"No," Hawke said. "We carry on to the compound."

Zeke shook his head. "We have to go help them, man!"

"We go on to our objective, Zeke. That's an order."

"I don't get it! They could be getting slaughtered over there!"

"Or it could be trap," Hawke said. "Maybe they're already dead, and Zamkov's men are trying to get us to walk right on over there for more of the same treatment?"

"We could at least check it out," Zeke said.

Hawke's voice grew harder. "We go on to the compound, is that clear?"

Zeke checked himself, and took a step back raising his palms. "It's your call, man. I said my piece."

Lea stepped up. "I know how you feel, Zeke. We all do, but Joe's right. It could be a trap, and meanwhile we're closer than ever to the compound. It's just another half mile over there."

She pointed behind her, then sighed.

Zeke stood down. "All right, you guys know what you're doing. I guess."

"There's no need to guess," Hawke said, feeling the heat. "We've done this a lot and we know what to do. Right now, Scarlet would tell us to go on to the compound. We're working in two separate squads, Zeke, and this one is heading out right now."

Hawke hefted his pack and slung his gun over his shoulder. Turning to shake Zeke's hand and show there was no hard feelings, he was stopped dead in his tracks by something over the Texan's shoulder.

Something that made his blood freeze in his veins.

"Fucking *hell*," he mumbled.

Lea's face dropped. "What is it?"

"It's some kind of robot." His voice was quiet, and dry.

She turned and saw it. They all did. Standing behind them in the path they had cleared was a four-legged robot. It was mostly black and chrome and covered in wires and tubes. The most clearly visible item was unmistakable – two grenade launchers fixed on its back.

Nikolai said, "It's seen us."

'Damn," Kamala said. "That thing is hideous."

"It's dangerous," Hawke said.

"Aww, don't talk about Robodog like that," Zeke said.

What served as a head now swivelled around and fixed what looked like a telephoto lens on them. A second later, both grenade launchers turned in their direction and the machine began stalking closer to them.

"How fast do you think that fucker goes?" Zeke said.

Kamala looked at him sideways. "What happened to *aww Robodog?*"

"I changed my mind. That puppy looks like it bites."

Nikolai frowned. "And we're about to find out just how hard – look!"

Then all hell broke loose as the machine leapt over a fallen log like a champion racehorse and took up a new position with a direct line of sight between itself and the ECHO team. Before anyone could speak, the first grenades began to fly.

CHAPTER NINETEEN

Half a mile to the west, a nine-mil bullet ripped right through the shoulder of Camacho's jacket and blew of out the other side in a cloud of blood spray and atomized leather. He smashed into the jungle floor at high speed and rolled in the black earth twice before stopping himself.

Reaper and Lexi set up a defensive perimeter, returning fire on the unknown shooters while Scarlet and Ryan rushed over to the wounded man.

"I told you to lose weight," Scarlet said. "You move like a rhino sometimes."

Camacho tried to smile through the pain. "You never complain about that in bed."

"Oh, *please*," Ryan said. "Spare me the grisly details of your love life."

Scarlet ripped off his jacket and checked the wound. "The round's long gone, but this is more than a flesh wound, Jack. Looks like it's quite deep."

Camacho clenched his hand and released it again, gritting his teeth in pain. "I can still move it, but yeah – maybe it feels a little weird."

Blood poured out of the wound and pumped over his shoulder, reddening his skin and rolling down into the dirt and leaves underneath him.

He looked up into her eyes. "So, what's the verdict, doc? Nerve damage?"

"I don't know, but we have to get it cleaned up fast. Ryan – get me Reap's bag right now."

He scrambled over to Reaper who was still firing on the men. The Frenchman shrugged the pack off and Ryan crouched low as he skidded back over to Scarlet through the dirt. "Here."

"Hold the wound shut."

Ryan gripped Camacho's shoulder while Scarlet searched the bag. She soon found what she was looking for in the legionnaire's survival kit – medical iodine solution, a roll of bandage and a tube of superglue.

She nudged Ryan out of the way and cleaned the wound. "Hold the wound together again, boy."

Ryan did as he was told, grumbling to himself about what she had called him as she squirted the glue along the top of the wound.

"Good of you *stick* with me, babe" Camacho said.

"At least living with Cairo hasn't destroyed your sense of humor," Ryan said.

Scarlet sighed as she worked. "It wasn't funny."

Camacho gasped in pain. "I thought it was!"

"You would," she said. "You said it."

"No, Cairo's right," Ryan said. "I was going to say how childish these puns are, butt fuck it."

"Very good, my young apprentice," Camacho said, chuckling through the pain "Very good."

"Ryan could pun in binary."

"Zero one one zero ze…"

Scarlet continued working on the wound. "Don't even go there."

"Ryan, I think you get ten points for that," Camacho said.

"Did you say points or pints?"

The bullets flew, flitting over their heads, shredding foliage and pinging off hardwood trunks, but Scarlet never flinched. When the glue was nearly hard, she wrapped the bandage around his arm, tight and snug and then tied it off. “You’ll live.”

“Thanks, babe. Hope I never have to return the favor.”

“We can’t hold them off for much longer,” Reaper called out.

“And I still can’t even see the bastards!” Lexi yelled.

Scarlet saw them first. Commandos in jungle kit, faces blacked out with camo grease and combat knives, bayonets and machetes in their hands. They moved like ghosts, fast and silent, leaping over the kapok roots into the clearing until they were almost upon them.

She called out to the others, but they had already seen the danger. Reaper swung his HK MP7 off his shoulder and pushed the stock into his hip as he aimed the muzzle at the enemy.

Letting rip with the gun, the gas-operated rotating bolt did its work, strafing the tropical foliage and raking hot rounds through two of the soldiers on their right flank. But they still came. As Ryan fumbled for his gun, Scarlet and Lexi saw the writing on the wall. The enemy was too close for a gunfight. Almost upon them now, these men were spoiling for hand-to-hand combat.

Both women pulled their knives just as their leader rushed Reaper from the side and kicked the submachine gun from his hands. The Frenchman kicked the gun into the undergrowth and wrenched a blade from the sheath on his belt.

Soldiers were everywhere. Lexi was hooking a man’s legs out from under him and elbowing him to the jungle floor. Scarlet lunged for one of the younger men, grabbing his wrist and pulling him toward her. At the same time, she used her other hand to deliver a sharp strike on his knife hand and knock the blade to the jungle floor.

He reached down for the weapon reflexively, but she saw it coming and brought her right boot up into his face. A wet, cracking noise indicated a broken nose and the man grunted in pain. He brought his hands up to his nose and growled in rage. Parrots squawked above their heads as Scarlet spun on the spot and swung her other boot around into the side of his head, knocking him out cold.

Moving in for the kill with her knife, she heard Ryan cry out. Turning, she saw one of the soldiers striking him in the face with a hefty back-handed slap. The hacker tumbled to the ground with a red mark on his cheek and temple, but his pride took the brunt of the assault. As the soldier raised his knife hand into the air and slashed it down at him, Ryan rolled to the side with half a second to spare.

The first three inches of the combat knife sliced down into the rich, black Amazonian earth and the soldier struggled to free the blade. Sensing that the tip of the knife must have cut down into the sprawling roots of the kapok tree, Ryan seized the moment. Leaping to his feet, he grabbed his own knife and lunged at the soldier.

But then he paused.

Stabbing a man in the back?

It felt wrong, even though the very same man had tried to kill him, and would still try to kill him as soon as he had freed his blade. And yet the young Englishman felt revulsed at the thought of ramming the knife through the man's back. He just couldn't do it, but the half-second of hesitation cost him dear.

The man had freed his knife and was spinning around. He rushed Ryan who took a step back and tripped over another of the kapok roots. He saw a white grin break out through the black camo paint on the soldier's face as he padded forward and raised the knife one more time.

And then the soldier fell to his knees and tumbled forward onto his face.

Ryan saw Lexi standing behind the dead soldier before he noticed her knife sticking out of his back. The Chinese assassin said nothing as she pulled the knife free and returned to the savage, close-quarter combat exploding all around him. He clambered to his feet one more time and snatched up his knife, cursing himself for his failure to take out the soldier.

A few yards deeper into the undergrowth, Reaper was brawling with the leader of the group, a broad, ugly man with a broken nose and cauliflower ears. Both men had disarmed each other of their weapons and were engaged in the bloodiest fist fight the young Londoner had ever seen, on or off the big screen.

And the former French foreign legionnaire seemed to be enjoying it.

Piledriving an iron fist into the commando's tanned, scarred face, he knocked him back through a wall of lobster-claw plants and sent a disturbed monkey frog leaping for its life from one of the leaves.

Then everything changed, and in a hurry. Another wave of soldiers arrived from the south – this time more heavily armed. A well-worn man in jungle fatigues approached them, slowly but with a gun in his hand. The soldiers they were engaged with broke off the fight and took a step back as this new man stepped up to the ECHO team. Behind him, they saw a drone hovering just below the canopy.

"Who is the leader?" he asked.

"I am," Scarlet said.

He looked her up and down and smirked. "My name is Machete. You know what happens now."

Scarlet visibly deflated, dropping her knife to the jungle floor and raising her hands. The odds of taking the

Brazilians out were better than even, but the killer drone changed everything. With that on their side, Machete and his men were never going to lose.

Lexi was next, cursing wildly in Mandarin before letting her knife fall at her feet. Ryan followed her, letting his blade slip away from his, bruised, bleeding hand.

Machete saw Reaper was still holding the combat knife in his dirty hand. "What about you, big man?"

The two men stared into each other's hate-filled eyes for a few seconds before the inevitable. When Reaper dropped his knife, he spat into a nearby rattan palm and uttered a vow of revenge in low, mumbled Provençal.

"Now, you come with us. No talking. No trouble. Any problems and we'll put a bullet through this one's head." He grabbed Ryan by the scruff of the neck and then pushed him away again. "Or maybe I'll put that bullet through his stomach and let him spend the night bleeding out in the jungle."

Scarlet ignored the threat. "Where are you taking us?"

A greasy grin appeared on Machete's pock-marked face. "Nowhere you want to know about in advance. Now, move."

With guns trained on them and the mighty Brazilian sun piercing through the canopy and burning their necks, they marched along the narrow path. Trained in jungle warfare, Scarlet soon noticed that the track was very well maintained.

In this sort of climate and ecosystem, no manmade path would last longer than a few seasons before being completely swallowed by the jungle. Here and there, she saw other pathways cutting through the undergrowth. Someone was deliberately keeping a network of these paths clear, and it didn't take a genius to work out why: they were for the robots.

"Are these tracks for your little Wall-E friends?"

"It doesn't concern you," Machete said. "At least not yet."

Carneiro laughed. "Not yet. That's funny."

They reached a small lodge in the middle of the jungle. Raised on stilts to avoid flooding in the wet season and with a thick woven palm thatch, it looked like the sort of accommodation offered by a holiday company specialising in tropical retreats.

Machete marched them up to the entrance and told them to stay where they were. He and his men simply left them standing outside while they went up into the lodge. Confused, and with their clothes slick with sweat and stuck to their exhausted bodies, they took a few seconds to consider the situation.

"What the hell is going on?" Ryan asked.

"This has been on my mind, too." Reaper wiped sweat from his forehead and scratched his greying temple. "But whatever it is, they marched us in the opposite direction from the compound, so we're even further away from Hawke's team than before."

Lexi raised an eyebrow. "You mean, if we need to rescue them?"

Ryan scanned the trees surrounding the lodge. "I wish I could find that funny."

Machete emerged from the open doorway and made his way down the wooden steps at the front of the lodge. "Okay, I just spoke with the boss."

A long silence. The rest of his men assembled at the top of the steps, guns slung over their shoulders and cigarettes hanging from lips.

Scarlet put her hands on her hips. "And what does the boss say?"

"He says you're most welcome here on the mesa, and he has a special surprise planned for you."

"Don't tell me," Scarlet said. "He's providing a lodge just like this one with a Swedish masseur, a full body exfoliation and a hot tub?"

"The lodge you got right," he said with a grin. "But it's a very different type of lodge, much more hospital than this one."

Ryan looked over at Camacho and lowered his voice. "What does he mean?"

"Come," Machete said. "Mr Zamkov is meeting you soon, and he's not a man to be kept waiting."

CHAPTER TWENTY

The Dove walked casually along one of the many paths criss-crossing the vast compound, momentarily turning his aviator shades up to the blue sky. With his fashionable blue jeans and a crisp white shirt reflecting the Brazilian sun, he looked more like a model who had just stepped off a catwalk than the right-hand man of Nikita Zamkov.

His chiselled good-looks and tanned face aside, *o Pombo* was at this moment probably the most dangerous man in the Amazon basin. Born to a single mother in the favelas of western Rio, back when they were even more dangerous than today, he had learned from an early age how to defend himself. Nowhere offered a bleaker life to a child than the streets of Vila Aliança, but he had navigated its brutal treachery with courage and guile.

His childhood was not the normal one of love and encouragement and learning, but a savage test of endurance. A time of broken bones, split lips and cracked knuckles. A time of drug traffickers and blackmailers and thieves and killers. To protect his beautiful mother, he had fought with men twice his weight and three times his age.

And won.

For the Dove, his childhood was a testament to his strength.

But it had set him on a certain course in life, a sad, unchangeable course. At twelve he started stealing from tourists walking along Copacabana Beach, or those enjoying drinks in Ipanema, or taking photos in front of Cristo Redentor.

Christ the Redeemer, he thought, but there can be no redemption for a man like me.

Might as well impress the devil.

He took in the staggering skyline of Zamkov's compound, white, clean, and surrounded by the mesa's tropical wildlife, and he wondered what life really would be like after Eschaton. Better, was his first thought. The slums of his younger days would be cleared in the same way he used to pour petrol on cockroach nests and set them on fire. But it wouldn't stop there. The Butcher had big plans. When all this was over, the world would never look the same again.

"Perhaps I will move into the Alvorada Palace," he mused. "If it's good enough for the president of Brazil, then it's good enough for me."

He continued along the path. Ahead of him, a number of scientists in their white lab coats strolled along another path, chatting amiably in the sunshine as they made their way to one of the labs on the south side of the compound. It was not an area he was overly familiar with, in fact, he wasn't even sure if he had the necessary security clearance to get into it.

And that was just fine with him.

He'd seen the biohazard warnings on the doors leading down there and he'd heard the screams, too. Where Zamkov got his victims from he had no idea, but he suspected they were a small part of the vast number of people who went missing every year in Brazil. Snatched off the streets, taken away from their lives and their loved ones, only to be brought to a place like this, and then…

It didn't bear thinking about, and that really meant something coming from the Dove. He had knifed men, strangled women and blown up families, but what the Butcher was doing in the restricted area 66 made him stop and think about humanity.

He made his way up the steps into the nerve center. When he walked into Mission Control, Zamkov was busy talking with the American defense contractor. He approached them, just catching something his boss was saying.

"You're talking about KAIST?" the Russian asked.

Moran nodded. "Yes, the Korean Advanced Institute of Science and Technology. They work in conjunction with the country's second largest weapons manufacturer, Hanwha Systems."

"I am perfectly aware of that, Jackson. Hanwha systems are good, but many, many years behind our work here at Vyraj."

The Dove watched the American drum his fingers on the desktop, unsure what to say next to his host. "They're very controversial."

"Are they?"

"Why, of course. Just last year dozens of academics and researchers from all around the world organized a boycott in protest of their work on killer robots."

"I am aware of this, too. The boycott was implemented in protest of KAIST's partnership with Hanhwa and their explicit goal of developing killer robots. Note the word explicit. It seems like it's perfectly ethical to develop killer robots, just so long as you don't tell everyone that's your goal."

Zamkov laughed at his own comment, but the Dove noticed Moran was starting to look even more unsettled than he usually did.

Moran found his voice and spoke up. "KAIST issued a reassurance that they would be good boys and not create an army of Terminators any time soon."

A smile grew on Zamkov's face. "Does that reassure you?"

"No, you?"

"I don't care what they do. As I say, they are years behind me, if not decades. Happily, my work here would not be affected by silly games like boycotts. What KAIST and Hanwha, or even the covert US projects might achieve by 2040 is already alive and kicking right now and right here, in Vyraj."

Zamkov's eyes began to glaze over. "Military drones unimaginable to regular science today, AI killer robots that would look like something out of a Hollywood blockbuster to anyone alive today… but stop looking so concerned, Jackson. This is why you're here, is it not? To buy a little army of Terminators for your government?"

"It is."

"To fight the Russians?" Zamkov said with a smirk.

"Buying the weapons systems from you is one thing, but telling what our plans are with them is quite another. That's classified."

"Or the Chinese, maybe?"

"Classified."

"Ah! I know what you want them for, how could I have been so stupid?" Zamkov sipped his vodka and fixed two laser beam eyes on Moran until he looked away. "You need this army of AI killer robots to keep your own population under control! Am I right, or am I right?"

"I…"

"All that wargaming in your little government bunkers has finally spat out the terrifying conclusion you all dreaded – your country is collapsing, just like mine. More debt than can ever be paid back. A fractured economy dependent on imports of products created by slave workers in the developing world. Increasing disaffection with the government."

"As I say, it's classified."

"Don't worry, Jackson, and don't take it personally. For many years, all my most lucrative clients have been governments buying AI systems to suppress and monitor their own peoples."

"Can we move this along?"

"And yet, none of them have ever asked why it has proven to be necessary, that they need to deploy weaponry like I create on their own citizens. But fear not, Jackson. Fear not. Very soon, all of these problems will be solved."

"And what does that mean?"

Zamkov set the vodka glass down on the table with a light chink. "I've said too much. Ignore me – I am a humble technocrat whose stomach has been warmed by too much vodka. I am talking nonsense. Perhaps this might be a good time to see a demonstration of the systems you are purchasing?"

The Dove noticed that Moran was almost out of his chair before Zamkov had finished the sentence. "Just show me the way."

"I think you'll enjoy the show."

CHAPTER TWENTY-ONE

Machete marched Scarlet and her team to a large clearing a few hundred meters south of the lodge where they had made them wait while contacting Zamkov. Stepping out of the jungle and into the blazing heat of the Amazonian day was an eye-opening experience, especially for Ryan who had been struggling with the weather since their arrival.

Now, he had his men line them up in front of a much larger and vastly superior hunting lodge, and keep them under guard while a Lockheed Cheyenne helicopter swooped over the canopy. It flew in low over their heads and touched down on the clearing just behind the lodge. Scanning for an escape route, Scarlet noticed something off to their right. It was the size of a small family car and covered in a black tarp. Beyond it, at the far end of the clearing, she now saw the metal bars of a cage flashing in the sun. Looking closer, she was horrified to see people inside it.

She nudged Camacho's arm. "Check that out."

He turned and looked. "Jesus."

As the men from the helicopter came nearer, she sensed a frisson of anxiety ripple across Machete's unit and then a small group of men walked into sight. With the sound of the chopper's rotors still whirring, she counted four new people. The one in the middle had to be Zamkov, and beside him was an overweight man with an American military crewcut – Moran? On the other side was a tall, tanned man in a white linen shirt and the face and build of a supermodel, and then there was another man beside him. She didn't know why, but something was definitely off with the last one.

Maybe something about the way he walked, or the look in his eyes.

"Check out that lot," Ryan whispered. "You think one of them is Moran?"

Scarlet nodded. "Fat guy in the suit, for sure."

Then, followed by the small party, Zamkov ascended a series of wooden steps and addressed them from the lodge's veranda.

"Why are you on my land?"

"We were looking for exotic butterflies," Scarlet called out. "But we found you, instead."

"My men say you had weapons on you. Again, why are you here?"

"You have no right to hold us prisoner."

"I have every right. This is private land and you are spies."

The Russian spoke privately with the others on the veranda, then turned back to the prisoners out in the sun.

"You have made a mistake coming here today. Here, you will face an enemy you have no chance of defeating. You will see weapons that you could not until now imagine. They will terrify you. They will make you question what it means to be human. You will fight bravely, I know, but you will all die. Remember this, it is a privilege to die in this place, and in combat with my creations."

"This guy is as crazy as a packet of broken crackers," Ryan whispered.

Zamkov gestured at a soldier, who stepped off the veranda into the sun. He walked around to the tarp and pulled it away to reveal a heavy-duty piece of military kit.

"This is the latest model in my AI sentry gun range," Zamkov said proudly, though more to Moran than Scarlet. "It features an uncooled infrared thermographic optical system which uses special pyroelectric materials to locate human body warmth through not only dense undergrowth, but also through most modern buildings."

"Amazing."

"And the laser rangefinder mounted onboard is years ahead of anything currently on the market. It can track targets moving at any speed, and is linked to the infrared illuminator via a cutting-edge weapons interface. Until now, this has only been dreamed of."

"Impressive. How much does this cost?"

"Each unit is a quarter of a million dollars."

Moran gave an appreciative nod. "A fair price. What about the business end?"

"It's armed with a 50mm light machinegun with a rate of fire of over one thousand rounds per minute. It could turn this lodge into matchwood quicker than you can think about it. And for those hard to reach pests, we also incorporated a 50mm double-action grenade launcher. It fires six grenades per second from a rotary drum magazine."

Moran whistled. "Six grenades per second?"

"Laser targeted."

Scarlet and Reaper exchanged a concerned glance. Each of them understood they had no chance against a weapon like this even in the best of circumstances, but in a place like this, their chances were less than zero. And like the others, they were feeling dizzy and weak. Standing in the sun for so long with no water to hydrate themselves had taken its toll.

Moran had been considering the sentry gun, but now he turned to the Russian with a question on his face. "But what about these Z-bots you talked about in the chopper on the way over here?"

"The Z-bots are not for now," he said quietly. "This particular scenario is beneath their capabilities. Perhaps we will see them after we have dined."

"You told me the price of each unit was one hundred and seventy-five million dollars. That's even more than our most expensive fighter jet, the F-22 Raptor. Whatever the hell it is, it must be very impressive."

"You have no idea."

"Sounds intriguing."

"The Z-bot, or the Zamkov AIKR Mark IX, is my finest work, but now I want to demonstrate these other fine systems."

"I understand."

Down in the clearing, an exhausted Ryan started to collapse. Reaper caught him by his upper arm and held him up straight. "Hold on for a bit longer, mon ami. This will be over soon."

"I need some water."

"We all do. Focus on something in the distance and think about your most treasured memory."

"Thanks, Vincent."

The Frenchman leaned into him. "We're on a mission, but just this once, I'll let you call me that."

Scarlet, who had heard the mumbled conversation, felt the corners of her mouth turn up. If a situation as hellish as this had a silver lining, it was in its power to bring the people she loved even closer together. Her mood changed rapidly when she thought about how Ryan was going to deal with the terror ahead of them.

Since the early days, he had done a lot to improve his fitness and stamina, and she had a vague idea of how Maria's murder had toughened him up, but the jungle was a hard place to fight in. He had no training, and he was already severely depleted by the trek. She felt herself shudder when she realized he was unlikely to survive the day.

Maybe they all were.

Above them, in the lodge, Zamkov shouted and snapped her back into the moment. One of his soldiers responded by activating the sentry gun. Its matte black metal turret spun around and raised itself a few inches above the main body. The muzzle rose and fell and turned a full three-sixty degrees until fixing on the small group of men and women in the cage on the far side of the clearing.

"Surely not," Scarlet said.

Lexi looked on through the shimmering heat haze, through the grasses blowing gently in the over-hot wind, and studied the faces of the captives. "Now it all makes sense. Shorten was right after all – this place is nothing but a hunting ground. That sick son of a bitch Zamkov uses his slaves as live targets to test his latest weapons systems."

"And we're the latest targets," Ryan said weakly. "Might as well paint a bullseye on my back."

Reaper clicked his tongue. "No more of that talk. We will win today just like we win every day."

"We have to run out of luck eventually." Ryan's voice was hoarse, breaking up with the dehydration. "Maybe we just ran out of road."

"Open the cage." When Zamkov spoke, it was casual, businesslike. "And release the prisoners."

Another soldier pushed a button and the cage door clunked out of its frame and slowly swung open. The prisoners looked at one another, confused, terrified. Then, one of the younger men made a break for it, darting out of the cage and running toward the tree line.

No one spoke. No one needed to. The sentry gun swivelled around and located the fleeing man in half a second. In an insane whir of hydraulics and metallic clicks and whines, the muzzle fixed on the man and tracked him as he ran through the trees.

"See the small screen," Zamkov said easily to Moran. "This is a live feed of what the sentry gun is seeing. You can see it has switched from regular light to infrared now he has tried to hide in the jungle. The truth is, it doesn't matter where he goes. There is nowhere he can run or hide where the S38 cannot find him."

With no warning, the light machinegun opened fire, barrel sweeping smoothly from right to left as the muzzle flashed in the burning sun. In a hail of shredded foliage, blasted tree trunk bark and squawking cobalt-winged parakeets, they all heard the wretched, blood-curdling screams of the man as he was cut to pieces and killed in the rainforest.

"You can see how effective this system is. He was half a kilometer away, hidden behind several meters of thick jungle, and yet the S38 was able to locate and track him in less than one second, and open fire, neutralizing the threat in less than five seconds."

"Threat?" Scarlet called up. "He was no threat, you sick bastard. He was a slave and you used him as nothing but a moving target!"

Zamkov shared a joke with the tall man in the white shirt, but the larger man she had presumed was Moran looked less amused. When the laugh was over, the Russian turned to Scarlet and raised his voice. "It is unfortunate that you came here today, but now you will share the same fate as the others here."

Ryan started to slip again. "He can't be serious?"

Reaper held on to him a second time. "Stay on your feet, mon ami."

"I will now count to ten," Zamkov said. "Then I will order two things to happen. First, I will send my commandos after you, and second, I will order the sentry gun to kill you. This way we can test the gun against jungle-trained killers." He turned to Moran. "The commandos have never won."

"I'll kill you for this, Zamkov," Camacho said.

The Russian waved his hand in a dismissive gesture. "Now – run like silly, frightened rabbits. This amuses me."

"What about our weapons?" Reaper said.

"You can keep them." Zamkov shrugged. "Just makes it more fun."

Scarlet lunged forward. Soldiers aimed guns and Camacho pulled her back.

"You can't do this, you bastard!" she cried.

"Ten…"

She saw Camacho's eyes looking into hers. "He's not screwing around, babe. We have to get out of here, right now!"

"Nine…"

"We can't just run like scared animals!"

"This time, we have no choice." Reaper said this, and now he was pulling Ryan's arm up over his shoulder and moving away to the tree line. "We stand more chance in there than in here."

"Eight…"

Scarlet knew he was right, and Camacho was already hooking Ryan's other arm over his shoulder to halve Reaper's burden. Swallowing her pride and putting her anger away for later, she joined Lexi and the five of them sprinted for the trees.

"Seven…"

As they pounded across the clearing, she heard the sentry gun's turret whirring around behind her. The sickening sound of hydraulics filled the hot air as it moved position on its tracks to get a better shot at them.

"Six..."

CHAPTER TWENTY-TWO

When Lea stopped rolling, she realized she had tumbled down a slope to the west of the path they'd been clearing. She hadn't gone far. There was too much vegetation dragging on her, clinging to her arms and legs as she slid away from the killer robot. Shaking the soil from her eyes and hair, she scanned the area for any sign of the others.

Above her at the top of the slope, she saw the section of the jungle where they had been standing before the attack. It was still on fire, but there was no sign of her friends. Then she saw Zeke and Kamala to her left. They were higher up the slope and closer to the path. "Zeke!" she called out. "Have you seen Joe or Kolya?"

"They went the other side of the path!" he called back.

The sound of hydraulic legs powering the machine along the path filled the air. Lea fell silent. She knew what to do, but her pack was gone. It had come off further up the slope on her way down.

She crawled back up toward it, with one objective in her mind. Reaching out for the canvas strap, she dragged it down closer to her and opened the flap. "I know you're in here somewhere, ya little bastard… got ya!"

She pulled the grenade from the bag and then she saw it.

The robot was in the burning jungle at the top of the slope, looking back down at her. The lens it was using as an eye flashed in the dim sunlight, and then the grenade launchers swivelled around to her.

She fumbled for the pin on the grenade and then heard Hawke yelling. He was on the path now, and sprinting to the robot. Piling into it as if he might tackle a rugby player, he knocked the machine off its feet just as it was firing.

The grenades launched in the wrong direction, streaking up through the air and ripping through the canopy above. They exploded in the air and sent a small shockwave back down to their position around the path.

Lea scrambled to the top of the path, followed by Zeke and Kamala. When she reached the top, Hawke was still wrestling with the machine which was kicking and trying to right itself.

“Here,” she yelled.

He caught the grenade in one hand and pulled the pin just as Nikolai appeared on the other side of the path. After stuffing the grenade inside a gap in the base of the robot, Hawke screamed for everyone to take cover.

This time Lea found herself behind the trunk of a giant sumaumeira tree. Hawke was beside her, and when the grenade detonated, the explosion blasted the robot into a thousand pieces all over the jungle.

When the smoke had cleared, the team came out from their cover positions and looked at the damage. What had once been a lethal killing machine was no more than fist-sized pieces of metal, wires and circuitry scattered all over this small part of the rainforest. Most of the components were still smoking, and some were still on fire.

“That was close,” Zeke said.

“And where there’s one,” Kamala said, “there have got to be more, right?”

Nikolai looked shocked. “There will be more.”

Zeke clapped a hand on Hawke’s back. “Good work, man. We were nearly dog food back then for a second.”

Hawke didn’t reply. He had turned away from the smouldering wreck of the robot and was staring up into the sky where the grenades had ripped through the trees and created a new hole in the canopy.

Lea and the rest of the team looked at him. "What is it, Joe?"

"You hear that?"

"What?"

"Sounds like a siren," Kamala said.

Hawke shut his eyes and angled his ear toward the sound. "It's a klaxon, some sort of warning for something."

A low, deep rumbling shook the ground they were standing on. Leaves fell from trees and frightened birds left their nests, flying up into the clear blue sky.

"Is that an earthquake?"

"I don't think so," Zeke said.

Nikolai watched the foliage all around them tremble. "Do they even have earthquakes here?"

"Yes," Lea said. "They can have some pretty big magnitudes out here. Ryan made me watch a program on the Discovery Channel about it."

"But this was no earthquake." Hawke pointed his finger up at a break in the canopy. "Look."

They stared up at the small patch of cobalt blue high above them and saw the unmistakable sight of a rocket ripping into the upper atmosphere. Smooth, white and flashing in the bright sun, it cut across the sky at the head of a twisting exhaust trail. The upper part of the billowing plume was pink and orange in the sun, and then the rocket was out of sight.

"This is not good," Lea said.

Zeke sighed. "Please tell me that what I just saw is part of the Brazilian Space Agency?"

"I'm afraid not," Hawke said. "The agency has two launch sites, Alcântara and Barreira do Inferno. They're both thousands of kilometers away, out on the east coast.

Whatever we just saw take off was no more than half a mile away."

"And if it's not the BSA," Nikolai said solemnly, "that means that Zamkov has his own space program."

Lea followed the smoke trail as it drifted in the air. "Shorten said this place had launchpads."

Kamala passed a hand over her tired face. "And just when I thought this mission couldn't get any crazier."

"The question is," Lea said, "just what the hell does a man like Zamkov need with his own space program?"

"It's not so unusual these days," Zeke said. "Look at Elon Musk and Space X, look at Virgin Galactic, and there are a lot more private programs in Russia and China, too. It's not such a great leap to imagine a man like Zamkov having one."

"Maybe," Lea didn't sound convinced. "But those programs you mention are registered businesses that everyone knows about. Most of them are private companies working toward creating a profit and trading in the stock market – maybe by taking satellites up for nations or in space tourism. Last time I heard, there wasn't any private space program run by a man called the Butcher."

"I take your point."

"Lea's right," Kamala said. "This guy isn't developing technology for improving space tourism. Whatever the hell we just saw go up into space is secret, which is why he's using the world's most remote location to take it up there."

"Damn it all," Lea said. "We just need to get a hold of Jackson Moran! Now it looks like we have a whole load of other shit to handle too."

"Screw that," Zeke said. "We're here to get the Tartarus location from Moran, and after that we're out of here, right?"

All eyes turned to Hawke.

"No, not right," he said at last. "Yes, we need to get the location of Tartarus from Moran, but if there's anything nasty going on around here then we can't just ignore it. We have to live with ourselves."

Zeke gave an appreciative nod. "You're the boss, but things just got ratcheted up a few notches, wouldn't you say? When we started out on this mission, we thought we were breaking into some crazy dude's Bond villain bunker to snatch another crazy dude who knows were Tartarus is. Now it looks like we're up against a hell of a lot more."

Slowly, the birds began to return to their nests. The exhaust plume had dissipated in the upper atmosphere until it was almost impossible to see. For now, the sounds and sights of the natural ecosystem had been restored.

"Maybe we are," Hawke shrugged. "But it doesn't matter what we're up against, because whatever is waiting for us over there has to be faced down if we're going to rescue Alex. If anyone wants out, then all you have to do is march back to Tefé."

Zeke slapped Hawke on the shoulder. "I'm with you, chief. You guys saved my life back in Greece and I won't ever forget it."

"And I'm not going anywhere, either," Kamala said. "I have no life back in the States anymore. ECHO is my family now."

After the robot's brutal attack that had almost killed them all, Hawke felt invigorated by the show of solidarity. Whatever happened next, at least he knew he could trust those around him. "If Scarlet gets there first," he pointed in the direction of the compound, "we have to buy the beers, so let's get this done."

They laughed and hefted their packs and weapons.

Then they marched on, into the unknown.

CHAPTER TWENTY-THREE

Tracking the prisoners in the jungle was a cakewalk to Machete and his men. They knew this testing ground like the backs of their hands, plus, they had the sentry gun on their side. Zamkov was a strange man, but he paid well, and today he was paying them to demonstrate to the American that no matter how hard they worked, the AI gun would kill the targets first.

It was Machete's job to prove him wrong, but he had never done it. In all the years he had hunted targets around the mesa, the AI systems always terminated the target before he or his men could do it. It was an infuriating challenge, but he got paid one way or the other, so it meant less to him than he supposed Zamkov cared.

When they pulled up at the side of a clearing, he scanned the trees with heat-sensitive field glasses. "Looks like Zamkov is playing games with us and keeping the sentry gun back."

"He's a crazy bastard," one of his soldiers said.

Machete kept looking. "I don't see the prisoners."

"They went to the east," one of his men said. He recognised the voice. It was Carneiro, the newest member of his platoon.

"No, they would not go that way," Machete said. "They are ex-forces. You could tell by looking at them. They would go west. It's easier terrain."

He lowered the field glasses from his eyes and threw them in his pack. "We go west."

"No," Carneiro said. "They went east. I'm sure of it. Look at the broken plants."

"You're wrong. Now fall in line."

"But they went east!"

Machete sensed what came next. It had to happen. Like Carneiro, he knew a line had been crossed. Too much had been said. The younger man moved first, darting out a clenched fist and dodging to the left to avoid the response.

Machete reacted fast. His authority had been challenged by one of his soldiers and he couldn't let it stand. Order had to be maintained. Standing his ground, he blocked the punch and bunched his hand into a sold iron fist, ramming it into Carneiro's face and knocking him off his balance.

The young commando brought his right foot back and stopped himself from falling over. With his eyes fixed on Machete, he wiped his smashed mouth and spat a thick wad of blood on the jungle floor.

"You want to play it like that, huh?"

Machete said nothing. He knew more talk meant less fight. Staring right into his soul with the cold, unblinking eyes of a man who had lost count of how many he had killed, he beckoned him to attack again.

"You're a fool, Machete! You let that insane Russian treat you like shit! He treats us all like dogs and you say nothing."

"Fight me, or shut up," Machete said at last. "But if we fight, we fight to the death."

A shadow of doubt passed over Carneiro's sweating face as Machete pulled a blade and tossed it from one hand back to the other.

"Well?"

Before he could answer, they all heard the sound of a branch snapping to the west of their position. Machete resisted the temptation to say I told you so, and instead ordered his men to fan out and head over to the sound they had heard.

Without warning, a gunshot ripped through the foliage and cut down the man standing behind Carneiro. The platoon hit the ground, readying weapons and peering through the vegetation to find the gunman.

"Over there!" Carneiro said. "At one o'clock!"

Another gunshot, this time taking out a second member of the platoon. Machete fired back, and the rest of his men followed his lead. A vicious fire fight ended seconds later when they hit one of the enemy. It was the younger man, and Carneiro's shot had sent him spinning around like a top.

"Good work, Carneiro," Machete said. "Maybe you're not such an asshole, after all."

Carneiro was grateful for the grudging compliment. "Thanks, boss."

"Let's move in for the kill."

*

Thanks to her SAS days, Scarlet knew how hard a jungle fought back. Any battle in this environment meant you had two enemies – the soldiers and the landscape. Now, with Ryan down with a bullet wound, she ordered the others to return fire and hold the enemy back while she went back to being a nurse for the second time that day.

"Am I going to die?" Ryan croaked.

Scarlet breathed a sigh of relief when she saw the bullet had done no more than grazed the right side of his skull. A line of burnt hair and blood stretched from his temple to the back of his head and he was in serious shock, but he was essentially unharmed.

"Only if I kill you, you idiot."

He raised his head. "But it hurts like hell!"

"It would do, plus having a round pass that close to your ear isn't the best of experiences. It's a piece of flying metal going nearly two thousand miles an hour, after all."

"In your accent, you make it sound almost alluring."

"Stop being a prat. Like I said, it missed. I wouldn't have."

A massive explosion thumped the air behind their position and Reaper and Camacho shared a high five. The American turned and winked at Scarlet. "We just took out the sentry gun with a grenade."

"That's something. Now you just need to get Machete off our backs and we're good to go. The boy here isn't badly hurt."

Ryan craned his neck and twisted his head to face her. "You mean I'm going to be all right?"

Scarlet ducked as a ricocheting round pinged past her head. "You were never all right, boy."

"I see nothing's changed between us. That's something."

"It still has to be cleaned. You can't leave a wound like that in a place like this." Scarlet reached into her bag and found a half bottle of vodka. She unscrewed the cap and slopped some of it on the gash across his head. "The alcohol in here will help kill some of the germs. It's not a proper disinfectant, but it's better than nothing."

"What about the iodine?" he said.

"Used it up on Jack. Now, shut up and don't bite your tongue because this might hurt."

"I bet you haven't said that since the first night you slept with—

His sentence was cut short with his own scream as the vodka splashed down into the deep graze on his head. Looking up, he saw Scarlet grinning at him.

"You were saying?" she said.

"Thanks, Cairo."

"Don't think this comes easily, boy." She shook the empty bottle. "I was looking forward to this."

"I owe you one."

"One hundred, maybe." She tied some fabric torn from her shirt around the wound and tossed the empty bottle back in her pack. Slapping him on his shoulder, she gave him a rare smile. "All good?"

"All good."

The others were still engaged in a heavy exchange of fire with the other soldiers, and in the distance, she heard more soldiers running along one of the cleared pathways. "They must have split up into two squads. We're up against the wall, Reap."

"You don't have to tell me," he called back. "But we're very close to the compound."

She got to her feet and readied a weapon, but Reaper also had good news. "We just picked another two of them off. They're good – very good, but we are better. We're driving them back."

Scarlet aimed her weapon and fired on the retreating men.

"They've stopped firing," Reaper called out.

Scarlet heard what he said, and then they all heard a ghostly silence in the woods.

Why had things gone so quiet? Her mind raced as she considered the possibilities. Moments ago, the commandos had struck like lightning. Bursting out of their position and attacking them without warning, they had fought hard but had been driven back. Gone to ground with no counteroffensive? To Scarlet, this didn't seem likely. There had to be another reason why they had dropped off the radar.

She looked to Reaper and they shared a knowing look. "It's got to be air support."

"For sure," Lexi said.

Ryan scanned the canopy. "Sounds like trouble."

"If you think it *sounds* like trouble, boy, then wait till you experience the real thing," Scarlet said. "Get ready to clutch your pearls because this is going to get nasty."

"How nasty?"

"Very – it's a classic," said Scarlet. "You pull your men out so they don't get killed when you start bombing and strafing from the air."

Camacho agreed. "And knowing what we now know about Zamkov, the air support around here is going to be pretty damned ugly and twice as fast, right?"

Then they heard a buzzing noise echoing in the treetops.

"Killer drones," Lexi called out. "Somewhere north of us."

Ryan clambered to his feet. "We need to get of here, right now!"

CHAPTER TWENTY-FOUR

With one eye on the Butcher, Moran lifted the phone to his ear and took the call from Washington DC. The news was good. Jack Brooke and his daughter had tried to escape, but they had been located at the base's perimeter and taken back into custody. The Secret Service agent Brandon McGee was dead – shot and killed defending them in the escape attempt.

No loss there, he thought. "All right, thanks Josh."

Josh Muston cut the call and Moran slipped the phone back in his pocket.

Zamkov peered into his soul. "You seem pleased, Jackson."

Moran shifted uncomfortably in his seat on the veranda. "That was the President's Chief of Staff. There was an escape attempt from an important facility we call Tartarus, but the prisoners are back in custody."

"Well, that *is* good news." He turned to Yakov. "Where is our food?"

"A drone landed a few moments ago, sir."

"Good."

In the distance, Machete and the surviving members of his team emerged from the tree line and walked across the tree line to the lodge. Their exhausted, sweat-stained bodies shimmered in the heat haze, and when they reached the shade thrown on the ground by the lodge, Moran saw their faces and arms were covered in cuts and bruises.

"You lose to my technology, yet again."

"They're good, Mr Zamkov," Machete said. "Not like the usual ones. They took out the sentry gun and killed four of my men."

Zamkov nodded. He didn't seem displeased at all. "Then we must rise to the occasion, sergeant. I have already ordered a fleet of my new killer drones into the jungle. That is why you were ordered to retreat." Turning to Moran, he lowered his voice to a confidential tone. "Of course, you of all people are aware that the entire development of delivery drones was simply a way to desensitize people to their existence, ready for when they are converted into killer drones."

"Of course."

Zamkov shrugged. "And my killer drones are at least ten years ahead of those in the United States at this time, as you would expect. Now, we eat." He addresses Machete now, without turning away from Moran. "Sergeant, you and your men go and clean up."

"Sir."

As Machete and the soldiers padded away, defeated but not broken by the intruders, the Russian set eyes on a servant carrying a tray of food from the inside of the lodge out to their position on the veranda.

Moran's piggy eyes sparkled as the servants set the plates down and removed the cloches, then when he registered what he was seeing, he had to fight the smile on his face from turning into a rictus of disgust. "Looks… *delicious*. What is all this stuff?"

Zamkov took his time, relishing every item in front of him. "This is marbled Wagyu beef, and this is delicious pork sashimi made from kurobuta pork served with dashi jelly, and here we have raw chicken gizzard strips and grated ginger and soy sauce. If you had only visited last week, you could have sampled a fine dish of basashi –

raw horsemeat served with shoyu and grated ginger. My chef really surpassed himself with that one."

"Sounds… incredible."

"Indeed," Zamkov said, missing the sarcasm. He lifted a piece of the raw meat and studied it for a few moments. The sheen of the fresh blood, glossy and smooth in the cool light, pleased him. After rotating the fork a few times, he slipped the flesh into his mouth and savored every bite.

Moran watched in disgust as the Russian turned the meat over in his mouth, chewing every last ounce of flavor from it and then swallowing. As it slid down his throat, a curious smile spread on the Butcher's thin lips.

"Won't you join me?"

He raised a hand, palm out. "Not for me, thanks."

"It's an exquisite taste. The rawness makes it so soft, so smooth. After you have tried it, the idea of chewing cooked meat becomes repulsive."

"Really, I'm good."

Moran had watched an old boss of his gobble up a steak tartare once, back in Georgetown following a long meeting with another defense contractor. It was a well-known dish, but that had still turned his stomach. This, on the other hand, was something else altogether. These were strips of tenderloin an inch thick, the sort of thing you might give to a dog for a treat if you had more money that sense. Watching the pale Russian consume them with such enthusiasm made him feel sick.

Zamkov drank some cabernet, swilling it around his mouth for a few seconds before swallowing. "Raw chicken is even smoother."

Moran wanted to retch, but made an effort to hold it together for his host. To say a lot was riding on the outcome of this meeting was the understatement of the year – his career, for one thing, not to mention the future security of the United States.

"Have you ever sampled such a delicacy?"

"I can't say that I have," Moran said.

In the background, somewhere over in the jungle, Moran heard the sound of the aerial killer drones going to work. The *ratatatat* of automatic gunfire and the meaty bass thuds of grenade explosions echoing above the steaming canopy. Someone in there was having a hell of a hard day. Every now and then the ground shook with the impact of the detonations, but Zamkov was absorbed with his meal.

"Yes, the chicken is smooth like silk. It just slides down the throat."

The DIA man was certain eating raw chicken was a seriously bad idea, and how the Butcher had gotten away with it for so long, he had no idea. Words like campylobacter bacteria and salmonella swirled in his mind and he felt his stomach turning again.

"I have all my meals prepared from freshly slaughtered animals. We keep them right here in the compound. Right here in Vyraj. All killed-to-order. Have a look around the farm and select anything you desire. We're raising bullfrogs."

Moran raised a quizzical eyebrow. "You're raising bullfrogs?"

"They are a great delicacy eaten in many Asian countries. Enjoying them raw with a little soy sauce or perhaps garnished with a little shredded daikon is exquisite."

Moran thought he was going to be sick. "That's… good to know."

"This new chicken sashimi recipe created by my personal chef is out of this world. He got the recipe from a Japanese colleague in Osaka. Did you know that chicken tartare is on the menu in several restaurants in Japan?"

Keep it together, Jackson. "I did not know that."

Then, out of nowhere, the Russian fired another question at him. "Tell me, where is this Tartarus?"

"That's classified."

Zamkov stopped chewing the beef and turned his, small grey eyes on Moran. "You are here to discuss the most lucrative defense contract in American history, Mr Moran. Surely you must be able to tell me where it is."

"I cannot, no. Not without clearance from the very top of the US Government."

"You disappoint me."

"I'm sorry, sir, but that's just how it is. Tartarus Base is ranked at the very top of the black site list for secrecy. It has to be that way."

Zamkov was not offended. "Perhaps I will make knowing its location integral to the contract, if I so desire."

"That's well above my paygrade, sir. I'm merely here to check the weapons systems and facilitate that part of the deal. If you want to change the terms of the contract, then that is your right. You'll need to contact the head of the DIA to start that process and he'll take it to the President."

Zamkov sucked another piece of the raw meat buffet into his mouth. This time it looked like a slice of the chicken gizzard. "We will see, but right now I am not concerned with it. I was just curious. My only real interest lies with the technology I have surrounded myself with."

"Which is above impressive."

The Russian nodded absent-mindedly. "I know you are impressed. Everyone who comes here is impressed. Being so far ahead of anything being done in the rest of the world, including the most cutting-edge military black projects of the United States or China, is inherently impressive, after all."

Moran felt the atmosphere change. It had happened when Zamkov had said the word China.

"Tell me, sir. Are you in talks with the Chinese about supplying them with any of your technology?"

Zamkov gave him a cold smile. "That's classified, Mr Moran." Seeing the disappointment on his face, he continued. "I'm sorry, but that's just how it is. The work done here in Vyraj is ranked at the very top of my secrets."

Moran got the message and returned the smile with a fake one of his own. "Touché."

"Now." Zamkov set down his fork, wiped some blood from his mouth and finished his wine before pushing away from the table. "Perhaps you would like to see some of the work we have been doing here in closer detail?"

Moran finished his wine and nodded. "That's why I'm here, sir. Just lead the way."

CHAPTER TWENTY-FIVE

Even though he was the slowest in the team, Ryan Bale never knew his legs could move so fast. He pounded each footfall down into the black leafy earth with everything he had, desperate to keep up with the other much fitter members of the team. Behind him, the drones pursued them with only one objective: to kill them all, stone dead.

Camacho was right in front of him, and then Lexi and Scarlet at the front. Reaper had volunteered to take the rear, thank god, and was firing on one of the aerial killers right now with a handheld grenade launcher.

"How we doing, Reap?" Scarlet yelled.

They all heard the Frenchman curse.

"That good, eh?"

The difficulty wasn't his aim but the speed with which the drones could fly out of harm's way. Grenade after grenade sailed past them and exploded in the jungle behind. They had counted six of them when the attack started and so far, only managed to destroy four. With two more circling above them, they were far from being even halfway safe.

"I think they have cluster munitions!" Reaper yelled.

The lead drone weaved through the canopy and around a tree trunk before increasing speed and divebombing Ryan. It opened fire with savage intensity, its AI brain selecting the machinegun this time and not the grenades. Fifty mil rounds raked through the dirt and leaves in the jungle beside him and drilled into the ground inches from his boots.

Ryan nearly jumped out of his skin, swearing and cursing as he tucked his head into his shoulders and dived down behind the nearest trunk. His head wound radiated pain and he rolled to a stop in the earth. To his left, Reaper turned and fired, this time hitting the lead drone with a grenade and blasting it to pieces.

Scarlet tucked herself behind a trunk and thumbed the magazine release on her weapons. The empty mag clattered to the floor and she smacked a new one inside the grip.

"I hope this isn't one of those fucked up situations that cannot be unfucked!"

"I hear ya!" Camacho called back.

She fired on the other drone with her submachine gun, staying cool and aiming a few inches to its left. Knowing it would alter course to avoid the bullets, she now flicked the gun's muzzle to the left and made contact with the main body as it swerved into the path of the flying rounds.

"And that makes none," she said, resting the smoking muzzle on her shoulder.

Camacho brought himself to a wheezing heap beside her. "Good shooting, babe."

Now, Lexi, Ryan and Reaper joined them. All were out of breath but grateful to be alive.

"Zamkov *has* to know we survived that," Ryan said. "They had cameras on board. He was probably watching it live."

"He'll send Machete back out," Lexi said.

"Whatever he decides to do, he can only hit us if he knows where we are," Camacho said. "I say we get going to the compound and get this damned mission over and done."

Ryan's breathing was slower now. "I vote for that."

"No – wait," Scarlet said. "Zamkov knows we didn't come here for the wildlife, right? He knows we're here to hit the compound, and he knows where we are right now. If we take the most direct route there from here, he's going to find us in seconds. I hate to say it, but the smartest thing we can do right now is head out to the west for half a mile or so before heading toward the compound from a totally new direction."

Lexi and Reaper immediately agreed.

Ryan and Camacho shared a weary look. "Sounds like a great idea," the American said. "I could use the extra exercise."

"What about you, boy?" Scarlet said. "Coming along?"

Lexi looked at the young man's face. "Aww, it's not that much further. Turn that frown upside down, grumpy guts."

"All right," he said at last. "But only because you asked so nicely."

They started to move away, and Reaper moved to pick up his pack. As he yanked it up off the ground, the strap caught on something and snapped tight. He narrowed his eyes and was careful to stop pulling. Anyone else might have given it an extra hard tug, but the first thing that had come into his mind was *boobytrap*.

"What's the delay, Reap?" Scarlet said.

"I see something – a handle, hidden in the leaves at the side of the path."

Scarlet stopped dead in her tracks and reached for her weapon. "What is it?"

Everyone gathered around the bag as Reaper crouched down and carefully cleared the leaves away with his hands. Finding a leather strap fashioned into a handle, he checked it over and then gave it a pull, revealing a trapdoor. He got to his feet and pulled his water canteen from his pack.

"Et voila."

"Woah," Ryan said. "That's kinda groovy."

"What the hell is it?" Camacho said.

Reaper took a slug of warm water from his canteen and wiped his mouth with his tattooed forearm. Without looking at her, he handed the canteen to Lexi. Dropping to his knees once again, he peered down into the hole in the jungle floor. He lowered his voice into a grumble and said, "Synthétique, certainement."

"What did you say?" Lexi asked.

"It's manmade," the Frenchman said. "Without a doubt."

Hope and caution flickered on the Chinese assassin's face. "Like the *Cu Chi* tunnels?"

"I think so."

"You mean the ones used by the Viet Cong during the Vietnam War?" Ryan asked.

"Exactement, but they were dug much earlier, during the 1940s in the war of resistance against the French. My grandfather was there."

"I never knew that," Scarlet said.

Shrugging, Reaper said, "We need to know where this thing goes."

Ryan took a double take at the former legionnaire. "You're not seriously suggesting we crawl down into that thing?"

Reaper turned his square, unshaved face up to the much younger man. "And why not?"

"I'll tell you why not, because we don't know what the hell is down there! For all we know it's another one of Zamkov's little robot runs! You want to be trapped down in a tunnel barely big enough to squeeze into when a killer robot comes around the corner?"

"*Or*," Scarlet said patiently, "it's a tunnel system created by the people Zamkov has been hunting. It might even lead us inside the compound and we can hook back up with Joe and the others."

Reaper nodded at some unspoken thought and then climbed down into the tunnel without saying a word.

"Looks like we're going underground, boy."

Ryan rolled his eyes and sighed in frustration. "Why does nobody listen to me?"

Scarlet went in next, and Lexi wrapped her arm over his shoulders. "You know, the Viet Cong soldiers could locate one of these hidden trapdoors, open it, get inside and close it again, with all their equipment and guns, in just a few seconds. How long will it take you?"

"Why do you ask?"

"Because if you're not faster than me you'll be last."

Ryan's eyes widened at the thought of being at the rear down inside the tunnel, and the terror increased as he imagined a killer robot trundling around a bend in the darkness and aiming as his back. Five seconds later he was climbing down behind Scarlet, leaving Lexi shaking her head up on the surface.

At the base of a short vertical shaft, Reaper flicked on his Maglite and shone the beam down the tunnel. Lexi's observation had been exactly right – it was eerily similar to the tunnels used by the Viet Cong during the war.

Back then, the American soldiers had called life down in the vast tunnel network the *black echo*, such was the terrible conditions when living underground inside the labyrinth. Soldiers of the National Liberation Front lived in the filthy tunnels, with poor access to clean water and food. Venomous creatures like spiders, snakes and scorpions crawled through the humid darkness, and malaria and intestinal parasites were commonplace.

Shining his flashlight to the right, he saw another vertical shaft dropping away even deeper. Just like the

Viet Cong's tunnels, it looked like whoever had dug this network had created several different layers.

Working hard to keep his bearings, he followed the original tunnel straight ahead, reckoning that it was leading in the direction of the compound. In the damp darkness, time seemed to slow almost to nothing as they made their way through the underground system.

"When we get out of this jungle," Lexi said to break the silence, "I'm getting a bath and a long, cold drink. What about you guys?"

"I'll join you in the bath," Ryan said. "But I'm trying to trim down, so I'll say no to the drink."

Camacho laughed and Lexi slapped the back of Ryan's head. "That's not what I meant."

"I'm sure I'll find something to do," he said, chuckling to himself.

"You never know," Scarlet said. "there might be a code written in binary for you to solve."

"Woah," Ryan said. "Way to turn my floppy disk into a hard drive!"

"Oh, *please*," Scarlet said.

"What? Don't you want me to upload some data into your cloud?"

She turned and went toe to toe with him. "I think I just threw up in my mouth."

Reaper called their attention. "I hate to break this up, but it looks like we have got a choice to make."

They had reached a T-junction at the end of their tunnel. The Frenchman swept the flashlight beam from left to right and studied both new tunnels. Then, in the periphery of his vision he saw the faintest of lights flickering in the tunnel on the left. Shushing the team behind him, he advised them of what he had seen.

"You think it's more fucking robots?" Scarlet said.

"Non," he said quietly. "I hear voices, murmuring. I think it must be the people we saw being hunted earlier today. Maybe you were right about this being their tunnel system."

"There," Ryan said, pointing. He was standing at the back of the group and peering through the gap between Reaper and Camacho. "I see someone."

"But someone else saw you first, meu amigo."

He felt the cold metallic muzzle of a gun pushing into the back of his head, and then the low, gravelly voice continued.

"All of you will lay down your weapons and turn very slowly, or I *will* kill this man where he stands."

With the cold steel on his skull, Ryan was first to drop his gun and raise his hands.

CHAPTER TWENTY-SIX

To the east, Hawke and Lea ducked down just inside the tree line and studied the compound's enormous perimeter wall. It was at least fifty feet high and manned guardhouses on the top of the wall gave Zamkov's soldiers a look-out every hundred meters or so. To reach its base, they had to cross twenty meters of flat wetland which offered no cover at all.

"That's one hell of a perimeter wall," Hawke said, handing the monocular to Lea. "And it looks like Shorten wasn't having us on about the security. Looks like we've got to get past a twelve-foot-high razor wire fence first."

"With pressure pads between the fence and the wall," she said.

Hawke scouted the top of the wall far beyond the fence. "But it wouldn't be fun without the pressure pads."

"We've had easier jobs," she said.

The others reached the tree line and crouched down beside them. "Still no word from Cairo on the radio," Zeke said. "And holy crap, look at the size of the wall."

"Just what we were thinking," Hawke said. "And don't worry about Cairo. She can look after herself. Now, it's diversion time. Lea, Zeke and I are going to make a break for that wall. Kolya and Kamala, we need you to draw the fire of the guardhouse. When we reach the top, we'll neutralize the other guardhouses on this stretch of the wall and then you climb up and join us. All good?"

Nikolai gave a grave nod. "I can do what you ask."

"What about you, Kamala?" Lea asked.

"Count me in. When we've got their attention, we should run along the inside of the tree line to the west. The terrain is easier that way."

"Sounds like a plan," Zeke said.

A truck trundled along a road winding along the base of the wall. It pulled up at the gatehouse and the driver spoke to the soldiers posted there for a few seconds. The truck was battered and dented with chipped paint and mud sprayed up the sides. In the back, under a soft canvas top, Hawke counted the terrified faces of at least six people. The soldier spoke into his radio and the boom gate lifted. By the time the truck had reached the main gate – two heavy steel doors – they swung open and it drove inside the compound.

"I hate to say it, but it looks like Shorten was right," Lea said.

The atmosphere grew darker, and Kamala looked at her in horror. "You mean what he said about the experiments?"

Lea nodded. "I think so, and I think those people are headed to Zamkov's labs."

"I was hoping that old pilot had gotten his facts wrong," Zeke said. "But now I think you might be right. Did you see the looks on their faces?"

"They must be from some of the smaller communities we saw along the river when we flew in," Hawke said. "If they came from further afield, they'd have been flown into the airfield, just the way Shorten described. Maybe Zamkov told them there was work here at the base, or maybe he just had them kidnapped at gunpoint. Who knows? Either way, we're going to have sort it out before we leave with Moran."

"Wait, we're taking that dude with us?" Zeke asked. "I thought we were just going to beat the information out of him, Bauer-style."

Hawke gave him a look. "Bauer-style? Moran is a top DIA officer with more interrogation resistance training sessions than you've had hot dinners. My guess is, he won't tell us what we need to know without considerable persuasion, and that means removing him to a safehouse where we can work on him in peace."

"Work on him?" Kamala asked. "You mean torture?"

Hawke fixed his eyes on her. "We need to know where Tartarus is, Kamala."

She backed down, giving a simple nod of agreement. "I know."

For a moment, he'd wondered if she was going to raise a serious ethical objection to what had to be done to Moran, and it reminded him of Kim Taylor. She had been in the ECHO team since the mission against Klaus Kiefel and his insane plan to attack the United States with a bioweapon derived from the remains of Medusa.

Murdered in cold blood by the unknown sniper, Kim had always stood by her ethics and argued against the torture of suspects. A nostalgic smile turned the corner of his mouth up as he thought about the many arguments he'd had with her over the years. She had been a tough, determined and yet caring member of the team.

The sniper would have to pay for her death, too, along with the murders of Danny and Magnus.

"All right," he said at last, "this is it. We need to get on. You okay with that, Bauer-style?"

Zeke laughed and nodded. "Let's roll!"

Kamala and Nikolai sprinted through the jungle on their way to cause the diversion. The others waited silently in the humid thicket until they heard gunfire crackling off to their right. Hawke glanced up at the guardhouse and saw the soldiers scrambling in response. Most fired their rifles into the trees while others barked into their radios, alerting the other soldiers in the next guardhouse along.

"That's our cue."

As the bullets ripped through the undergrowth and shredded the leaves and vines in their pursuit of Kamala and Nikolai, Hawke, Lea and Zeke broke cover and sprinted toward the base of the wall.

Out on the cleared wetland now, they were horribly exposed as they pounded along the marshy land, bags of equipment slung over their shoulders. Above them, Zamkov's soldiers were still busy firing into the trees. Startled by the unexpected intrusion and finally with someone to shoot at, they had abandoned their other duty of guarding this part of the perimeter just as Hawke had hoped, and this allowed them to reach the base of the wall unharmed.

Slamming his back up against the brick, Hawke slipped his bag off his shoulder and reached inside for a rocket-powered grapnel. Time was of the essence if the three of them were to secure the ropes and climb to the top of the wall before the soldiers gave up on the wild goose chase and returned to their duties.

Hawke fired the grapnel and the hooks dug into the stone at the top of the wall. Gripping the nylon rope with climbing gloves, he tested it was secure and then began to walk up the wall. The strong sun and high humidity made the climb a tense minute of hard work, but he soon reached the top and slipped over a crenelated ridge to find himself on a narrow gangway. The nearest guardhouse was still empty, and the soldiers were still out on the wall to its west, busily engaged in the diversion.

"All clear!"

Lea was next, easily ascending the wall and joining him, and Zeke made three.

"That was crazy!" the Texan said. "But nowhere near as insane as this place – take a look!"

The enormous compound stretched away to the south. Resembling a large town built on a grid system, roads intersected blocks of concrete buildings, and to the west they saw the airfield the Canadian bush pilot had described.

The base's soldiers were billeted in accommodation blocks close to the southern perimeter and the main gatehouse where formal visitors arrived. The organization of the place staggered Lea. She had known her fair share of military bases over the years, but this was the biggest and most lavishly funded military complex she had ever seen.

At their backs, they heard more shooting. Hawke turned his head and saw the soldiers firing on Nikolai and Kamala once again. "We have to stop them."

Charging the next guardhouse, Zeke easily disarmed his opponent, and then used the heavy stock of the rifle to knock the man out. Behind him, Lea smashed a palm strike into a soldier's throat and sent him tottering back over the edge of the wall.

"Remind me never to get into a disagreement with you!" the Texan called out.

Lea spun around and engaged with the next soldier. "I'll do just that, Zeke!"

The fight lasted seconds. The ECHO team's surprise attack had combined with the diversion to give them the advantage they needed to overwhelm the guards. Stepping over the unconscious guards, they left the guardhouse and stared out over the wall. "Where are they now?"

"I see them!" Lea said. "They're over there – Kolya in the lead. They're tracking back just as planned."

They watched as their two friends sprinted across the wetland and climbed up the same nylon grapnel ropes they had used moments earlier. Gathered together at the top of the wall, the five of them made for the guardhouse, once again stepping over the unconscious bodies of the soldiers as they went.

Zeke was breathing hard. Getting himself together, he rummaged around in his pack and grabbed another mag. Ejecting the spent one from his weapon, he smacked it into place before turning his bright eyes up to the others. "Last one, guys."

"We can steal more as we make our way through the compound," Hawke said, sighting his gun on a building and scanning the area ahead of them for any sign of enemy soldiers. "We can use the massive size of this place against Zamkov. We move fast and shoot out any CCTV every time we see it."

They heard a tinny voice, crackling in the guardhouse. A quick investigation turned up a radio on the belt of one of the unconscious soldiers. Hawke reached down and unhooked it from the man's belt.

"What are you doing?" Zeke asked.

"Getting them off our backs."

"You speak Portuguese?"

"No, but I speak Spanish. That's enough to get the job done."

Kamala looked doubtful. "I hope you're right."

Hawke thumbed the push-to-talk and activated the transmitter. "Falso alarme."

More talking, obscured by static.

Hawke replied one more time. "Falso alarme." Turning off the transmitter, he tossed the radio to the ground. "Hope that does the trick."

"I don't hear any alarms," Kamala said.

Nikolai stared at the radio, unconvinced by Hawke's language skills. "Yet."

Shrugging it away, Hawke pulled the slide on his gun. "All right, let's move."

CHAPTER TWENTY-SEVEN

Scarlet and the others had been walking through the tunnel system for a quarter of an hour. The unknown gunman was still at their backs and their hands were still raised in the air. When she saw a dim orange glow emanating from a small hole in the wall, the man behind them ordered them to stop.

"What now?" she called back to him.

"Now you crouch down and go through the hole."

She started to turn around. They all did.

"Stay where you are!" His voice was full of anger.

Turning back to the hole, Scarlet said, "It's just that it doesn't look all that inviting, and I learnt as a child never to climb into holes you couldn't see into."

They heard the sound of a hammer being pulled back on the handgun. "It's much more inviting than a bullet in the back of your head. Get in the hole."

Scarlet couldn't disagree with the man. The hole option seemed altogether better than the alternative, so she crouched down and crawled through towards the amber light. Lexi, Reaper and Ryan followed. Camacho was last, and by the time he got to his feet it was just in time to see the rest of his friends standing in awe at the view.

The man crawled through next and waved the gun at them. "What are you waiting for? Please, go and get something to eat and drink."

Scarlet stared at the underground cavern in amazement. It was around the size of a small theatre, its walls were marked with other holes and larger tunnel entrances, and at least a dozen dirt-smeared people dressed in rags sat around on rocks, talking and eating from a simmering pot over a fire in the center of the cave. The smoke from the fire drifted up to the cave ceiling where it vanished into several tiny slits.

When the man with the gun saw her staring up at the smoke, he laughed. "You're wondering why Zamkov doesn't see the smoke?"

"As a matter of fact, yes."

Ryan said, "It must come out somewhere near the boiling river. The steam disguises the smoke, am I right?"

"You would survive here," the man said. "You are very clever. You have to be clever to survive here. Most die within days." He stuffed the gun in his belt and offered him his hand to shake. "My name is Eduardo."

"I'm Scarlet. This is Ryan, Lexi, Jack and Vincent."

Reaper sighed. "Bonjour."

Eduardo nodded and gestured to the pot. "Please, I meant what I said. It's fish stew today. The fish is fresh. Caught in the river over our heads a few hours ago – but not the boiling river," he said with a grin.

They accepted the offer and sat on logs positioned around the small pot. Eating from clay bowls, they found it more than passable given the circumstances and very soon the conversation turned to the terrible way these people were living.

"I'm presuming you're all escapees from the compound?" Scarlet asked.

Eduardo gave a casual nod and spooned more stew into his mouth. "Aren't you?"

"Actually no. We want to get *into* to the compound, not escape from it."

Eduardo was astonished. "Then you are crazy in the head."

"You can say that again," Ryan said.

"But *why?*" Eduardo asked.

Camacho spoke next. "We need to speak to a man inside."

"Not Zamkov?"

"No," said Scarlet. A long pause. The fire crackled and someone behind them coughed. "I can't tell you. You could be anyone."

Eduardo gave a deep belly laugh. "You have done what no one has been able to do for weeks – put a smile on my face. Yes, you are right. I am one of Zamkov's spies. I live down here in the filth and eat insects, but he pays very well."

Scarlet looked at his eyes and saw the pain. "We're looking for a man named Jackson Moran. He's an American government official working for the DIA."

Eduardo gave a sage nod. "There are lots like your man. They fly in and out of the jungle like birds. They buy weapons from here. Very, very bad weapons."

"Like the ones that hunted you up *there*," said a gaunt man who now came and sat beside Eduardo.

"How did you get here?" Reaper asked.

Eduardo turned to the man beside him. "This is Paulo. He had been down in the tunnels the longest. Perhaps he will answer."

"Some of us were kidnapped," Paulo said in a pathetic whisper, his voice barely audible above the sound of the crackling fire. "Others came to work in the compound voluntarily. We all end up his slaves one way or another, and when we make a mistake or get too old to work fast enough, we're taken out to the jungle in a cage and hunted by his systems. He uses us as living targets so he can give more reliable data to his clients."

Eduardo saw his friend start to break up and took over the story. "If any of us survive, we are taken back to the compound and locked up, or made to work again. Then, when the next weapon is ready, we are brought back out to the jungle. Years ago, Paulo here, was being hunted by a robot when he fell down a hole and into one of the mesa's caves. He had escaped the robot, but there was no way out… until he climbed up the roots of a tree and made his way back up to the surface."

"It was then I had my idea," Paulo said. "As I was climbing up the roots, I saw the soil changing as I got closer to the surface. You see, I was a geologist before they kidnapped me in Manaus, so I was able to use my skills to identify a layer of clay and laterite much closer to the surface. It's very common in tropical areas like this and similar to the clay the Vietnamese dug their tunnels in during the French colonial period."

Reaper and Lexi exchanged a glance. "We thought they looked similar."

"I studied history as a minor," Paulo said with a shrug. "Anyway, I tested it and knew it was soft enough to dig. Ten years later we have this network."

"You've been running for ten years?" Scarlet said.

"Some of us have been slaves for much longer. You would be amazed how much dirt you can dig out in that time. At least we are able to help others during the hunts. That was why I was in the upper levels of the tunnels when I found you. We heard the attack and I was on my way to open the hatch and try and get whoever was being hunted to safety. When I saw your weapons, however, I had to take precautions."

"Does Zamkov know you're down here?" Ryan asked.

He shrugged. "Maybe, maybe not. Perhaps he's developing a new AI system to hunt people underground and wants to keep us here for testing."

The sad, desolate words hung in the air.

Scarlet set her bowl down and looked Eduardo in the eye. "How extensive are these tunnels?"

"Very."

"Are they mapped?"

He shook his head vigorously. "No. If Zamkov got hold of a map it would be over for us. The layout is in our heads. I already know what you're going to ask, and the answer is yes, yes and no."

The corner of Scarlet's mouth turned up. "And what was I going to ask?"

"If the tunnels go to the compound. Yes, they do, but only up to the compound wall, and yes, I will take you there, and no, we will not break the surface and go into Vyraj."

Scarlet felt an atmosphere of disagreement building.

"Why not?" Paulo said. "This is the chance we've been waiting for!"

"It's too dangerous," Eduardo said. "We've survived this long only by keeping out of sight. If you want to kill yourselves up there, then go right ahead, but don't take us with you."

"I disagree," said another man.

A woman stood up, her face lined with mud and scarred with scratches. "Me too. I say we go and fight." She raised her hands helplessly and shook her head. "This is not living, Lalo! This is the land of the living dead!"

Eduardo sensed the mood changing from one of passive indifference to something much more aggressive. He waved his hands to calm them, and then stood beside the fire. "We must *all* agree if we are to fight. Once we break the surface outside the compound and Zamkov's forces see us, there can be no hiding back down here. He will send his robots and his commandos down here and purge the entire system. We must think carefully."

"There is nothing to think about," Paulo said, getting to his feet. "I didn't know it when I woke this morning, but this is the last day I will ever live like this, down in a hole like vermin!"

The others cheered, and Scarlet and Camacho caught each other's eye.

"Looks like we just got ourselves a new team," the American said.

"Then let's get moving," Scarlet said. "I want this over and done with before nightfall."

CHAPTER TWENTY-EIGHT

When Eduardo finally opened the hatch at the end of a long march through the tunnel system, everyone was grateful to see daylight and breathe fresh air again. After the ECHO team climbed to the surface and checked the coast was clear, Eduardo led his own small band of survivors out of the tunnel and into the hot, humid jungle.

"Which way, Eduardo?" Scarlet asked.

He nodded to the south. "That way, a few hundred meters."

With both Ryan and Camacho suffering gunshot wounds, the small team marched south through the last section of jungle. Thick vegetation forced them to stop to hack a way through or change direction, but eventually they reached their destination.

The compound.

Their first glimpse of it was through a dense section of palm trees and hanging vines. They realized they were on slightly higher ground than the compound, but not high enough to see over the high walls running around the perimeter.

"Any guards?" Ryan asked.

Eduardo laughed bitterly. "Always."

"There." Reaper pointed to the top of the wall to the west. "It's a guardhouse of some sort. They seem to be posted every hundred meters or so."

Reaper used one of the vines to climb up the first few meters of a palm tree. "And it gets worse," he said. "I don't know if you can see from where you are, but you guys better get ready for Short Circuit again."

Camacho kicked a clump of dirt into the air. "Fuck it with a roll of dimes. I'm *sick* of those damned things."

Reaper scanned the area. "If we walk over there, we can have a better view."

He climbed down the tree and they moved over to the new position. He was right. A break in the vegetation and an even more elevated position gave them a clearer view of Vyraj's western perimeter.

And the robots.

"What the hell is it this time?" Lexi asked.

"It's another killer robot," Ryan said. "A hunter-killer."

"More AI?"

"Yeah, another LAW, but this time not airborne and significantly more advanced than the sentry gun."

"These things freak me out," Camacho said. "Wait – I see someone walking along the perimeter. It's one of the commandos from the fire fight earlier today."

They watched Carneiro walk along the perimeter and the LAW's turret spun around. With its sights fixed on the Brazilian commando, it tracked him for a few seconds and then stood down as he went inside the compound.

"Why didn't it take him out?" Lexi said.

"They utilize something called deep learning." Ryan crouched low as he peered through a monocular. "It's an AI capability which processes colossal quantities of data into an artificial neural network much like the human brain. In theory it uses this data to discriminate between combatants, to make sure it kills the enemy and not people on its own side."

"How reassuring," Lexi said. "Except for the fact that we are the enemy."

"Right, and using facial rec technology it knows that guy is a friendly. If his face hadn't been on the database in its neural network, it would have used that machine gun to spray him all over the perimeter wall."

"Thanks for that image," Scarlet said.

Ryan hadn't heard her. He was too busy staring at the robot. "Just think of all those learning algorithms and artificial neurons all whirring around and making it think, track, hunt… kill."

Camacho wiped sweat from his brow. "I'd rather not."

Scarlet was moving forward now, peering through the vegetation to get a clearer look at the thing as it trundled closer to them on its caterpillar tracks. "Is there anything we can do to shut these fuckers down?"

"No," Paulo said. "They are impossible to fight. We must get to the men behind the robots and kill them. That is our only chance."

"That's the best idea," Ryan said. "If we could get inside the compound, I might be able to hack the system and turn all of these AI robots against Zamkov, but it's a long shot. I'm guessing he's got things nailed down pretty hard in a place like this."

"Maybe we could exploit the fact it travels on tank treads," Reaper said. "By favoring certain terrain and so on."

"Problem is," Lexi said. "The terrain between our position and the wall is all flat."

They all saw the problem. The robots were patrolling up and down this section of the compound's wall which was a flat stretch of drained wetlands. Zamkov was no fool, and he'd selected this type of machine because it matched the terrain.

"But we could draw it away from the perimeter," Reaper said.

Scarlet's eyes darted over to the Frenchman. "You mean get it to follow us into the jungle?"

"It might not be programmed to leave its post," Ryan said.

"Or it might be." Camacho flicked off his safety catch. "And I think that makes it worth a shot."

Scarlet agreed. Crossing the perimeter with even just one of these things around was an impossibility. They stood no chance against what was, effectively. a miniature tank powered by the world's most advanced artificial intelligence. Unlike a flesh and blood opponent, there was no way they could take it out with a bullet. Its armor would resist any of their nine mil weapons and any attempt to take it out would simply alert it to their position.

"What about a grenade?" she asked. "You think it could take a direct hit from one of our grenades?"

"I think a direct hit might damage its treads," Reaper said. "And then it's a sitting duck."

"It's too far away to hit with a grenade right now," she said. "I say we lure the thing into the jungle and when it's close enough and on rougher terrain, we try and take it out with a grenade or two. That way, even if it survives the grenade, it's going to be caught up in all this vegetation."

"If it's programmed to leave its post," said Ryan.

"All right, we need some bait." Scarlet turned to Ryan. "Are you going to approach it from the west or east?"

His eyes opened as wide as saucers. "You are *shitting* me?"

"No, why?"

"Because I'm the IT guy and you lot are all ex-special forces!"

"Precisely." Scarlet checked her gun and pushed back from the vegetation. "We need all our best guns ready for when it chases you back into the jungle."

Ryan was still aghast. "You're not serious?"

"Look at my face."

CHAPTER TWENTY-NINE

Zamkov beamed at his latest fleet of predator drones as he showed them to Moran. "The latest American technology is the Pegasus X47B, a jet-powered drone capable of flying a two-thousand-mile range at Mach 0.9, just a tad under the speed of sound. In the Perun Z7R, I have developed a machine that makes the Pegasus look like the Wright brothers' flyer."

"That's an impressive claim." Moran wandered to the first drone and slid his hand over its sleek finish. "What allows you to make a claim like that?"

"The Perun – named after the Slavic god of thunder, naturally – is a weapons drone like no other. Its control center – its *brain*… is high frequency AI fusion software, which like most of my other creations here at Vyraj, writes its own programs. Unlike the latest American, Russian or Chinese machines, this drone is supersonic. Its service ceiling is over sixty thousand feet, its range is nearly ten thousand kilometers and it can carry over five thousand kilos of ordnance."

"Stealth, I presume?"

Zamkov laughed. "You disappointment me, Jackson." Turning to the drones and raising his voice, he said, "Perun fleet, invisibility mode."

Instantly, the entire fleet disappeared.

Moran took a step back and cursed. "What the hell?"

"Don't worry, the Chinese didn't sneak in and steal them all. They are all still exactly where they were, parked safely in this hangar. Similar to the Pegasus and other drones, they are equipped with an LED coating and cameras that film their surroundings live and project them to the aircraft's body. Only, instead of simply being along the bottom like in the case of the Pegasus, the Perun's entire surface…its *skin*, has the LED coating. Not only are they invisible to all radar, but thanks to my proprietary optical stealth technology, they are also invisible to the human eye."

"This is incredible." Moran took a step back toward where he had touched the first drone. "If the cameras are filming in the hangar and transmitting to the LED coating, how come it's not filming us – I mean, how come we're not visible in the image?"

Zamkov laughed again. "That's 2019 thinking. Jackson. I told you everything here at Vyraj is at least twenty years ahead of what you consider cutting edge research and development. On board each drone is an AI neural network, constantly discriminating between everything the cameras, or its… *eyes*, are seeing, every single attosecond."

"I don't understand – you're saying you programmed this thing to see through us?"

"Not exactly, and as I think I mentioned – this AI fusion software is not programmed by me – it writes itself. Right now, it has registered us and our location in this part of the hangar. Then, it has made a discriminating choice against us – classified us as a potential enemy – and selected specific cameras only to transmit what its eyes are seeing behind the drones as we see them."

Moran was stunned. "My God, it worked out we were humans, assessed our location and chose cameras that would film what was behind them from our perspective."

"In layman's terms."

"And you mean to say you didn't tell them to do this?"

"Not at all. Like all my AI creations, the basic Z1 warfare program was installed in them, with a few tweaks for each model, and then they write their own programs… they choose their own futures."

Moran looked unsettled again. "What the hell happens if they decide we're a threat?"

"If they had decided that, we would have been dead the minute we walked into the hangar."

"You mean you don't have the final kill decision?"

"No. I trust my creations totally. They are my children. The final kill decision rests with each of my units, and nowhere else."

"That's insane, Zamkov! That goes against every moral and legal code on earth. US law specifically states that the kill decision must reside with a human."

"Humans are overrated, my friend. Early trials already show that AI makes fewer mistakes in target selection than people. Everyone here on the base, including you, had a photograph taken upon arrival. You were also filmed."

"Yes, I remember."

"That data was uploaded into the main computer and from there taken into the central AI neural network. As far as my AI creations are concerned, everyone on that list is a friendly."

"You mean to say the only thing stopping these things going nuts and killing everything in sight is a simple facial recognition system?"

"Again, you underestimate me. This is no simple facial rec system, but the most advanced of its kind anywhere on earth. Right now, the AI in this room is watching your face, but it is also monitoring your height, weight, body shape, the way you walk, your breathing pattern and the sound of your voice. It knows who you are, Jackson, as well as I do. It's not just facial rec."

"Can you make them reappear?"

"Are they making you nervous?"

"You could say that."

"Perun fleet, visibility mode."

Once again, the fleet was before the DIA officer. "Thanks."

Zamkov's eyes sparkled as he took in the fleet, shimmering under the hangar's lights. "And yet, they are already being surpassed in my technical lab by the next generation, the Perun Z8. It's like watching your children grow up."

"Next generation? What the hell can they do?"

"You are not ready for that information."

Moran paused a beat, letting what he had seen sink in. "And you're saying that all of this technology is fitted to everything else around here?"

Zamkov nodded. "In one way or another, most of the AI units have a similar capability."

"Yakov, for example?"

"Yes, only I found it very hard to combine the flexible rubber skin and the LED coating, so his invisibility mode is not as good as the drones. I'm getting there, though."

Moran looked over his shoulder, half expecting the robot to be standing right behind him, partially obscured by invisibility mode. "How reassuring."

"If you think these are impressive, you are going to be blown away by the Svetovid Z13 LARs."

Moran looked at the Russian with a question on his face.

"Svetovid was the Slavic god of war. I gave his name to my army of lethal autonomous robots, or what I earlier referred to Z-bots. If you think these drones are dangerous, just wait till you meet the Svets. They make the latest Terminator movie look like Forbidden Planet's Robby the Robot, and if… Jackson? What's the matter?" You look pale."

"This is all far, far beyond our expectations, Nikita. We knew you were ahead – that's why I was sent down here to make the defense contract deal with you, but already what you've shown me is from another world. If you really do have an army of high frequency fusion software AI killer robots with this invisibility package, then… well, this is making me nervous."

Zamkov landed a heavy hand down on the American's back. "Just as well you're on my side then, right?"

As the Russian's laugh echoed in the hangar, Moran swallowed and gave his host an uncertain smile. "I guess so."

Yakov approached him and spoke in rapid Russian. Moran didn't catch a word.

"I'm sorry, but I have an important meeting and I must…" Zamkov paused, a mischievous look on his face. "Perhaps you would like to join me?"

"If it's a private meeting, then…"

"Nonsense," the Russian said warmly. "In fact, I'd like you to join me. I think it would be a turning point in our relationship."

"If you say so."

"You see, a member of my staff has been holding up production of my latest AI systems and today is his disciplinary. I'm sure you'd like to see how we do personnel management here at Zamkov Systems."

"Lead the way."

CHAPTER THIRTY

Hawke led his team behind the guardhouse and along the top of the wall until they reached a stainless-steel ladder inside a manhole cage. This was how the soldiers came and went to their posts, and peering over the side of the wall, he saw only a short distance between the base of the ladder and the nearest building.

The sun was directly overhead. His shadow was no more than a small pool around his boots and the ferocious heat of the jungle was rising. Visions of this nightmare being over seeped into his mind, but what everyone needed right now was Jackson Moran safely in custody. Relaxing in a shady pool with a cold drink would have to wait.

After one more quick study of the base below, he had made his route. "We go down the ladder, and use those buildings over there for cover. If we keep out of sight, we should be able to reach the main central section of the base in less than twenty minutes."

"And then?" Kamala asked.

"Then we find Zamkov."

"And if we find Zamkov, we find Moran," Lea said.

With the thought of cold beers and plunge pools still in his mind, Hawke slung his MP5 over his shoulder and climbed inside the manhole cage. He was halfway down by the time the others had got inside the cage, but they were all gathered on the ground below in no time at all.

The building closest to the wall was an ugly concrete block with a line of tinted windows running around its lower section. The tints meant there was no way to know if anyone was inside or not, but they were able to get to a pathway running around the outside of the building without anyone raising an alarm.

Here, in the shade of more palm trees, they regrouped before turning the corner of the building. The central superstructure of the compound was spherical and rose before them like a giant white golf ball flashing in the sun. Connected to all the other buildings by what looked like a monorail, Hawke knew at once this was where the action would be found. This was the central hub of the compound, and that meant Zamkov and Moran.

"That's our boy," he said.

Lea brushed past him, gun in hand and a flirtatious wink on her tanned face. "Then what are you waiting for?"

*

In the jungle outside the compound, Ryan Bale was once again sprinting away from one of the killer robots with all his might. For a vehicle on treads, it moved faster than any of them had expected, and when it started firing on him with the autocannon fixed on its turret, he dived into the cover of a giant banana tree.

Seconds after breaking through the enormous, shiny leaves, the robot tracked him into his hiding place, swivelled the muzzle to the right and ripped the leaves to shreds. The volley of fire was so aggressive it severed the trunk in half and felled the tree on top of him. Ryan saw what was happening in slow motion and rolled out of the way with seconds to spare.

The action never stopped, and before he finished rolling, he heard his friends opening fire on the robot. A hefty, deep explosion tore the heart out of the jungle's peaceful silence and then he saw a cloud of smoke and metal debris blooming in the air above him.

"Got the bastard." Scarlet's voice was loud and clear above the whoops of delight from the other members of the team. The men and women from the tunnel were especially overjoyed.

He got up, brushed the mud off and walked over to them. "To the wall, then."

"Good work, boy," she said.

The walk back to the compound's outer perimeter was short but draining. When they reached the tree line in front of the cleared land leading up to the wall, they stopped for more water and to wish each other good luck.

"What about those guardhouses?" Eduardo asked.

"Looks like they're not attended," Reaper said.

Camacho pointed to the left where thin black lines dangled down from the wall beyond the guardhouse. "Hawke got here first – see the ropes?"

Eduardo and Paulo shared a look. "There are more of you?"

"Sure are," the American said.

"And bugger them sideways, too," Scarlet said. "This means we lost." She turned to the others and frowned. "And the beers are on us."

Camacho kissed her on the temple. "Let's go get 'em, tiger."

Her pursed lips melted into a smile. "Race you."

By the time Camacho and the others were halfway across the cleared wetland, Scarlet was already walking up the wall, nylon climbing rope gripped in her gloved hands and a silenced pistol in her shoulder holster. Each side of her, the enormous wall stretched away, bending with the design of the compound until vanishing out of sight. Her new elevation allowed her to see further now, but the only view was endless swathes of wetlands and rainforest receding into the humid haze of the tropical day.

Beneath her, she heard Reaper fire another rocket-propelled grapnel up at the top of the wall. The steel flukes clawed into the brickwork, but the weight of the nylon rope pulled it back to earth. It scratched its way along the top of the wall until it got snagged on the raised lip running around the outside edge. Moments later, she reached the top. When the team was all present and correct, Reaper and Lexi returned to the bottom to help some of the weaker prisoners, but one by one they all joined her and surveyed the compound for the first time.

"What a pad," Camacho said.

"Oh là là," said Reaper. "C'est magnifique."

Eduardo shook his head. "It's terrifying."

"Ryan?" Scarlet turned. "You're unusually quiet."

"It's just that..." he pretended to break up. "I can't believe I finally made it to the set of Moonraker."

Lexi clipped him round the back of the head, accompanied by an eyeroll. "Idiot."

Before he could reply, they all jumped, startled by the sudden reactivation of their earpieces and the sound of Lea's voice.

"We've got comms back!" Ryan said.

"The jammer must be restricted to outside the compound," Camacho said.

Scarlet nodded as she fiddled with her earpiece "Makes sense. Lea, we're on site. Where are you?"

The Irish voice over the comms was urgent but controlled. "Glad you could make it, Cairo. Can you see the giant golf ball?"

"Yes."

"We're heading toward that."

"Received, over and – wait."

"What?"

"Can we make it that the last team to get to Zamkov buys the beers, rather than the last team into the compound?"

"No we bloody can't, you tight-arse."

Scarlet sighed. "Fine, we'll meet you there."

CHAPTER THIRTY-ONE

Sitting in the sun on the soft cloth seat, Jackson Moran had closed his eyes and let the monorail carriage's gentle hum and swaying motion almost lull him to sleep. When they arrived, he was nudged awake by the tall Brazilian, and then the small party, accompanied by Yakov, made their way into an outer hub. It was a large space, lit from above by bright Amazon sunshine streaming in through a glass atrium and below, a circular platform surrounded by real palm trees.

"Please," Zamkov said. "If you'll follow me."

They stepped off the monorail and walked down a gangway until they reached some sort of viewing platform on one side of the tank, just above the surface of the platform. Moran had barely taken his seat when he heard a man screaming for his life, and then he looked up and saw two guards dragging someone in a white lab coat toward the platform.

Something told him Zamkov's idea of personnel management was not what he had anticipated it might be, at all.

"Please, Mr Zamkov!"

Moran twisted his fat head. "What the hell is this, Nikita?"

"Meet Dr Grigori Shoygu."

Moran turned back and watched Shoygu as he struggled and kicked and tried to free himself from the men. He recognized the men holding him from the display back at the lodge. One was the older sergeant Zamkov had called Machete, and the other the younger man Carneiro.

"What is this all about? More weapons testing?"

Zamkov laughed. "No, not at all. This is purely for pleasure."

Moran realized he had started sweating in the cold, airconditioned space. Watching Zamkov release his slaves and hunt them down with AI weapons systems was one thing, but there was something even more sinister about the way the Russian had gathered his staff together and was forcing them to watch what was about to happen.

"I don't understand. Who is this Dr Shoygu? A member of your staff?"

"Not any longer," Zamkov said bitterly. "You see, here at Vyraj we are working many years in the future from the rest of the world. You know this now. Such an achievement can only be made with two essential ingredients. The first is my genius, and the second is the unquestioning loyalty and total dedication of my workforce. Dr Shoygu has not only questioned what we do here, but he has failed on multiple occasions to meet his deadlines. He is slowing me down. He is retarding the future of the world."

"I don't see how he…"

"And today, I am terminating his employment contract."

As he spoke, Machete and Carneiro dragged the screaming man up a steel dock ladder and threw him down on top of the platform. Looking closer, Moran saw this was a circular metal plate, surrounded by a corrugated metal wall. As Carneiro made his way back down the ladder, the sergeant slid a curved metal plate across the gangway, blocking any way out of what now looked like a sort of miniature amphitheatre.

Zamkov stretched his legs and leaned back in his seat. "People mistakenly say that they are carnivorous, when in fact they are omnivorous. They eat all manner of plants as well as meat."

"What the hell are you talking about, Mr Zamkov?"

Yakov was hovering at their side, and now Zamkov turned in his chair and gave him an order which made Moran's blood run cold.

"Retract the floor plates."

"Yes, sir."

Yakov threw a lever and only now did Moran see that the circular floor beneath Dr Shoygu was constituted of two semicircular metal plates. As they slowly slid apart, he saw a slit of bright blue water beneath him.

"We have LED underwater lighting, of course," Zamkov said casually.

"Oh my *god!*" Moran said. "Piranhas."

"You win a cigar, Jackson. Well done."

The metal plates continued to slide apart, and now a crazed, screaming Grigori Shoygu was desperately clawing at the smooth, curved metal panels running around the outside of the pit.

"This particular shoal was originally obtained from the Orinoco. They are particularly aggressive."

"Please, Mr Zamkov! Please sir!" The voice was hoarse and terrified, the man's bleeding fingers and bulging eyes said it all. "I'll do anything! Please, sir!"

"They are not actually as dangerous as most people believe unless you *encourage* them to be more aggressive. This is achieved here at Vyraj by keeping them in a very dense shoal and periodically starving them. I found out about Dr Shoygu's misdemeanors several days ago, for example, but kept him in his position until the fish were ready."

"This is insane."

Zamkov wasn't listening. "One day, I may create an even more efficient and aggressive AI version of the piranha, but for now these will suffice."

The wretched sight of Shoygu standing on his tiptoes on the last inch of plate was too much for Moran. The demonstration in the jungle was grim, but had taken place out of sight. Being forced to watch this got to him much more than he thought.

"I think you made your point, Nikita."

"Here he goes – watch!"

The last piece of the plate retracted behind the wall and Shoygu tumbled into the water. The reaction of the piranhas was savage. Moran had never seen anything like it. The water erupted as if a thousand jacuzzi jets had all been activated at once, and the desperate scientist was in the center of it all, squirming, screaming, taking water into his mouth and thrashing about like someone was running a million volts through him.

"It is fascinating watching them feed. They too, appreciate raw meat."

Moran fought back the nausea as he watched a blood-stained Grigori Shoygu break the surface, covered in the fish. So many hundreds of them were attached to his skin by their razor-sharp teeth, he looked like he was wearing some sort of suit.

His mangled cries were incomprehensible, and then they pulled him under the dark red-stained water, bubbling and frothy and nightmarish.

"Yakov, extend the plates."

"Yes, sir."

Zamkov sighed and dismissed the other staff members. "Sadly, their obedience and performance always picks up considerably after one of these shows."

Moran nodded, but found no words.

“Now, we must go to my mission control. If you thought that was impressive, you will not believe what I have to show you next.”

CHAPTER THIRTY-TWO

Hawke was pleased to see Scarlet and the rest of her team as they approached them in the shadows of what looked like some sort of laboratory. Running behind them were several men and women dressed in rags. Some held wooden clubs and others gripped rocks. They all had years of hatred etched deep on their faces.

"You're all right," he said. "Thank fuck for that."

"Why? Did you miss me, darling?"

"Yes, but I see you had no problem moving on. Who are your new friends?"

She looked back on the dishevelled crowd standing behind her. "It's a long story. Suffice it to say, they hate Zamkov a lot more than we do."

"That's good enough for me." He raised his arm and pointed at the giant white golf ball. "We think mission control is based in there."

Reaper started to speak when a low, rumbling roar ended his sentence.

"What the hell is that?" Kamala asked.

Ryan looked worried. "Sounds like something's happening on one of the launchpads."

"Bloody hell!" Lea said. "He must be going to launch more rockets."

"Did you see the one that went up earlier?" Hawke asked.

Scarlet nodded, but Camacho answered. "We sure did. I know Moran's a priority, but something tells me Zamkov's not sending up weather satellites. We have to put an end to whatever's going on here. Not just for their sake," he paused and raised his hand to Eduardo and his friends, "but for the whole damned world."

"Then it's a good job we came down to find Moran," Lea said. "Don't you think?"

The rumbling stopped and a large cloud of water vapor billowed up into the sky behind Mission Control. Hawke followed it as it bubbled up into the sky. "Yes, I think it just might be," he said. "And with the evening approaching, it's just about the perfect time of day for it."

"The perfect time of day for a relaxing bubble bath and a glass of sparkling wine, more like," Lea said.

Kamala sighed. "I hear that."

"We're breaking up into two teams again," Hawke said. "Scarlet's team goes and takes out the launchpads while the rest of us will storm Mission Control."

"Take out the launchpads?" Camacho said. "That's not going to be easy."

"Nonsense," said Ryan, glancing at Scarlet. "When it comes to destroying long phallic-shaped objects we have just the person on our team."

Scarlet moved to answer, but Hawke stepped in. "Those rockets aren't going anywhere with a grenade or two up their arses. Get on it. As for the rest of us, we'll go full on, right through the front door and shit all over this party."

They headed out, but Ryan was distracted.

"Ryan!" Lea said. "Get a sodding move on."

"He's still dreaming of the bubble bath and sparkling wine," Scarlet said. "He's trying to increase his masculinity."

"Piss off, Cairo," Ryan said. "As a matter of fact, I was trying to work out what the hell Zamkov is doing with the rockets."

"Whatever it is, it can't be good," she replied. "But at least we have the element of surprise."

A man's cry echoed in the air somewhere ahead of them. At first, it sounded like someone was in pain, then they realised it was a soldier on the balcony running around the top of the building at the base of the giant sphere. A second later, an ear-piercing klaxon filled the air all over the compound.

"Excellent," Ryan said. "That's us fucked then."

"We're on." Hawke gripped his MP5 and fired on the soldier. Raking him with rounds, he took his finger off the trigger and they all watched the dead man tumble over the balcony. He clipped the building's concrete roof, bounced and then hit the ground with a dull thud.

Then, a dozen more soldiers streamed through the door behind the balcony.

"Fire!" Hawke yelled. "Fan out, take over and fire! Advance on the target when you get the first chance."

A brutal exchange of gunfire opened between the two forces. Reaper broke cover and powered forward, bullets nipping at his heels as he smashed into the side wall of Mission Control and hurled a grenade up onto the balcony. It detonated a second later and sprayed dead soldiers and debris up into the air.

He screamed in French as Camacho and Ryan joined him and they used their submachine gun to fire on more soldiers now arriving from the west of the compound. Hawke and Lea advanced from the eastern end of Mission Control, while the others pushed forward from between the two.

The growling roar of gunfire never got any less terrifying, and it sounded like it was getting closer. Another fragmentation grenade exploded, blasting a hefty cloud of dirt into the air above a maintenance shed. The soldiers were well-armed and on home ground – and Hawke knew any hope of a covert infiltration of the nerve center was now long gone.

They had to keep going, though. He guessed Zamkov and his top brass, including Moran would have been alerted to their attack. Maybe they were rushing into a bunker or a panic room right now. That would make things more complicated. Reloading his pistol, with his back up against the wall, he watched Zeke and Kamala hurrying across the western end of the yard and skidding down behind the front wheels of one of the Gaucho utility vehicles. Further beyond, Scarlet's team was slipping away to the launchpads.

Lea peered around the maintenance shed, but pulled her head back in a hurry as a bullet pinged off the corrugated metal wall and ricocheted up into the sky. "Fuck me, that was close!"

"Christ, be *careful!*" Hawke cursed as more bullets from the guards up on the compound's roof pocked the ground behind them. "They have us pinned down, but they can't get the angle to take us out."

"And who says I'd let them take me out?"

They locked eyes. "And you say *I'm* the fool."

"No, I say you're an eejit. Different."

"If you say so."

"You know, I wouldn't mind taking *them* out."

"In three?"

"You read my mind."

They counted down and then each of them spun around their own end of the shed, guns raised at the rooftop. Unleashing a barrage of rounds on the soldiers, their kill rate was better than expected. They fired on different targets, gun extractors working overtime as they pulled the cases from their chambers and fired them out of the ejector ports into the bloody chaos. By the time they had made the cover of the entrance portico, four of the men had tumbled off the roof and crashed into the ground with lethal bullet wounds in their chests.

Lea winked at Hawke. "Not bad, even if I do say so myself."

"If that's how you take a man out, maybe I should rethink this marriage thing."

"Don't be such a big baby, Josiah. I'll be extra gentle with you, and you *know* it."

The rest of their team sprinted over to them and prepared to storm the building. Hawke laughed at Lea's joke and fixed some explosives to the door. "Take cover!"

They tucked down behind either side of the portico and cradled their heads as the explosion ripped out the door and blasted it all over the path.

"Let's go!" Hawke said.

They ran inside and saw more soldiers streaming down a flight of metal stairs. They looked like they led up to the rooftop. Firing on them, Hawke killed the first two and drove the rest back up the stairs to rethink their tactics.

"Forward!" he screamed to his team, waving his arm toward some double doors at the other end of the room. He was first through them and found himself on a raised platform looking down on a busy subterranean workspace. Men and women hurried around under the oppressive sound of the klaxon, some on foot, others in small carts.

Lea made a quick headcount. "They look like scientists."

"Christ, this really is like a Bond film," Zeke muttered. "Ryan was right."

"Zamkov has ideas above his station," Lea said.

Hawke counted over a dozen armed guards running into the warehouse-size room, all dressed in black boiler suits and gripping what looked like Veresk submachine guns. They streamed into the area like ants, each man knowing exactly where his post was and taking up a defensive position in seconds.

While he was tracking the enemy, he felt someone squeezing his hand. Without turning, he said, "I know you're scared Ryan, but this isn't appropriate."

"Now, what did I *just* say about you being an eejit?"

He turned and kissed Lea on the lips. "And you agreed to marry me. What does that make you?"

"Up there!" screamed a woman in one of the carts. The armed guards followed her screams and saw them now, standing on the upper level. From their defensive positions, they opened fire on them with a vengeance.

Hawke felt the rage of the attack smash into them like a shockwave. Bullets slashed through the air and bit into the concrete wall behind them. He hit the deck, smashing down on the steel plate of the walkway and covered his head from the stray bullets.

"This is another fine mess you've gotten me into, Josiah!"

"Why, thank you, Ollie."

She rolled her eyes as she swung her MP5 up from her side and tried to get an angle on the men below. The door behind them burst open and Zeke and Nikolai and the rest of the team flooded into the walkway, guns ablaze and war cries on their lips.

Hawke said a silent prayer and reached for a grenade. He pulled the pin and lobbed it across the antechamber at the men's defensive position. One of them scrambled to snatch it up but the fuse was to short and the explosion blew the man all over the other soldiers.

Another grenade detonated. Hawke spun around and saw Kamala had thrown it. Beyond her, Zeke and Nikolai made it around the walkway to the left and fired on the soldiers from another position, ripping them to pieces with the onslaught.

Then Hawke saw something that shocked him. Eduardo and the men and women who had been trapped underground, leaped over the steel rail at the top of the walkway and charged the last remaining soldiers. Screaming like wild animals as they rushed the improvised machinegun nest, several of them were cut to ribbons before Eduardo and Paulo climbed over the pallets and attacked the soldiers.

"Hold your fire!" Hawke yelled, desperately trying to stop ECHO from killing the friendlies with stray fire as they killed the soldiers. Rarely had he seen such anger as he watched the survivors of Zamkov's sick games tear the soldiers apart with their crude weapons.

With the soldiers no longer posing a threat, he and the rest of the team climbed down from the walkway and approached a blood-streaked Eduardo.

"Where is Zamkov?" the Brazilian asked, his chest heaving up and down.

Hawke saw the rage on the man's face. "We're dealing with Zamkov, Eduardo. Is that understood?"

"He must pay for what he has done to us!" Eduardo screamed.

"He *will*," Lea said calmly.

Then they heard Scarlet's voice on the comms. "Launchpads one and two are down, but better than that, we found what the boy calls an AI communications node."

"What is that?" Lea said.

"You mean what *was* it," Ryan said. "And the answer is, a critical piece of equipment sending commands from the neural network to many of the AI units across the base. Now it's on fire, a lot of Zamkov's AI is down and out."

"But not all of it?" Hawke asked.

"No," Ryan said. "He's got different AI systems running off of different nodes. Makes sense from a security point of view, plus I doubt he ever thought this place would come under attack anyway."

"Got it," Lea said. "Good work."

"Gotta go," Cairo said. "And just a heads up, you have more soldiers approaching Mission Control."

"Got it, Cairo," Hawke said. "Take the third rocket down and get over here as fast as you can."

"On it."

"Which way is the control room?" Lea said.

Pumped with adrenaline, Kamala lifted a trembling hand and pointed at some double doors behind the soldier's makeshift perimeter. "Right down there."

"Then we've almost got the bastards!" Hawke said. "Move forward!"

CHAPTER THIRTY-THREE

When Yakov had alerted Zamkov to the attack raging outside in the compound, the Russian had almost believed his robotic creation was malfunctioning. No one could attack Vyraj, especially those misfits he'd seen earlier out at the lodge. It was too well defended. His commandos were too dangerous. But then he heard the gunfire and the screams and the grenade explosions and realized Yakov was operating at peak efficiency, just as he had known deep in his heart.

Now, high on the main monitor in Mission Control, glowing blue pixels portrayed a plan view of the entire compound. The Butcher watched in disbelief as section after section turned red, each change in color depicting another part of Vyraj no longer under the control of his own forces.

What sort of a force could do something like this? At the very least, he considered, they must be facing several dozen and very heavily armed Special Ops forces. Fixing his eyes on Moran, his lip curled in disgust. "Is this part of the plan, Jackson?"

"What are you talking about?"

Zamkov nudged his chin at the screen. High above their heads the sound of the klaxon continued to sound from concealed speakers. "Wait until you've assessed all of my systems and then invade the place with American soldiers so you can kill me and steal my AI?"

Moran was aghast. "That's crazy! I don't know who the hell these people are, but I can tell you damned straight, they're not US."

Zamkov looked at him. Studied the well-paid bureaucrat with the fleshy jowls and tiny piggy eyes. "Then who are they?"

"I have no idea, but if this place was going to be raided by American forces, I would have been told."

"Maybe your government doesn't think you can be trusted."

"Nonsense. I have the highest clearance." He pointed at the monitors. "This is not an American operation, I swear!"

Zamkov mulled the words. Studied the fat man's eyes once again. "If you're lying to me, Jackson — "

"I'm not lying, dammit! And if whoever the hell this is gets in here, you'll see that when they kill me!"

Moran watched through the window in blood-chilling horror as an army of robots moved across the compound's grassy quadrangle. Their walking wasn't exactly human, but it was almost there, and much better than the latest work he had seen in the black ops programs up in the States. "My God."

"Yes, to them, I am their god," Zamkov said. "Now, they will defend the compound for as long as it takes, and even if…"

Zamkov's blood froze. Outside, the entire army had thundered to a halt. Now, the killer robots were standing on the spot, submachine gun arms dangling uselessly at their sides.

"What has happened?"

"Looks like your AI has a flaw," Moran said. "A fatal flaw."

Zamkov's eyes crawled over the stationary army and then back up into the control room. "I don't understand… they must have taken out one of the comms nodes."

Moran nudged his chin at Yakov. "Why is that still working?"

"*He* is still operational because he runs on an autonomous network, separate from the main AI fleet, as do all of my elite guard, but none of this should be happening!"

"Well, it sure as shit *is* happening, Nikita," Moran said. "So not only are we defenseless, but if we ever do get out of here, you can forget about the contract. If your AI can be neutralized in a local skirmish down here, right under your nose, then what good would it be when deployed all over the US, or against a foreign enemy? For all we know, your little robots could spring back to life and start firing on *us* any second. This is crazy."

Zamkov felt a deep, burning rage rising inside him. Vyraj had been his life, his whole reason for being, and now these people were destroying it and driving him away. He thought about what it would take for him to leave this place – what it would take out of him. His kingdom, his creations, all left behind. But whoever this was, they weren't here risking life and limb for nothing. They were here to kill him and steal his technology.

At least I have *Stavka*, he thought.

Then, the section nearest the control room turned red and he heard the sound of machine guns even closer now, and not just over the speaker system. Closing his eyes, he made the most difficult decision of his life.

"Yakov, come over here."

Moran stepped out of the way of the robotic personal assistant as it walked over to Zamkov.

"Yes, sir?"

"Initiate Operation Stavka."

"What is that?" Moran asked, panicking. "What is *Stavka?*"

"Stavka," Zamkov repeated. "The high command of the Russian armed forces during the final days of the Empire. It was the Stavka that ordered the Great Retreat in 1915. Now, over one hundred years later, I must make the same decision and retreat."

"Retreat where?"

Outside of the control room, they both heard the report of more machineguns and the sound of men screaming for their lives.

Zamkov raised a Grach pistol and pointed it at the American's chest. "That is not your concern, Jackson."

"What the hell is this?" He took a step back, eyeing the control console for anything he could use as a weapon.

"Stay where you are!" Zamkov shouted. "Yakov, get the helicopter over to the lab roof and have the jets prepare for take-off. I have an errand to run and then we're evacuating."

"Yes, sir."

"We're running away?"

"Wrong. *I* am running away."

Moran's eyes crawled over the burning rocket outside on launchpad three. "You can't leave me here!"

"Wrong again."

The gunshot was brutally loud, a single, metallic report like a metal tray crashing into a tiled floor. Moran saw the smoke twisting from the muzzle and then felt a warm, fuzzy pain in his stomach. The warmth turned much hotter now, and when he looked down, he saw a red rosette blooming out from a burnt hole in his white shirt, three inches above his waistline.

"Oh, *god*."

He looked back up to Zamkov, but the Butcher had already holstered the weapon and was busy barking Russian commands at Yakov. "And inform Barbosa, Rodrigues and the Dove that Stavka has been initiated and to meet me in Lab 7G. We'll go there via the escape tunnel."

"Yes, sir. What about *that?*" Yakov turned his head and looked at Moran.

"Mr Moran is a traitor and will die a traitor's death, bleeding out on the floor like a slaughtered pig in an abattoir."

The robot voice was chilling in the air. "Yes, sir."

"And ensure Grandfather is ready to go."

"Yes, sir."

The word *Grandfather* terrified Moran who now looked up, straining through the pain, and saw Zamkov and Yakov stand in front of one of the screens as it slowly moved up to reveal a hidden tunnel. He recalled Zamkov telling him all about Grandfather in their first meeting, and just thinking about it made his blood turn to ice.

"Please, not that," Moran said. "Anything but that."

Zamkov returned his plea with a sick smile.

And then he was gone.

CHAPTER THIRTY-FOUR

As the ECHO team approached the end of the corridor, two more fleeing soldiers turned the corner. They fumbled for their weapons, but Lea took them both out with her handgun. They tumbled to the floor, just the latest victims in a bloody battle. Behind them, Scarlet and the rest of the team assigned to the launchpads burst through the doors.

"All done?" Hawke asked.

"All three rockets well and truly neutered," Scarlet said with a raised eyebrow. "Just ask Ryan, he knows all about it."

Kamala looked confused. "What, being neutered or destroying rockets?"

Hawke broke into the banter. "At least whatever nightmare Zamkov was planning is officially over. Now, for the man himself."

Lea took a deep breath as she prepared for the final fight. "And Moran."

Gun raised into the aim, Hawke kicked open the door and found himself on a mezzanine above an enormous control room. He swept the gun from side to side as the rest of his team piled in behind him, but there was no sign of Zamkov. The only person in the room was Jackson Moran, and he was moaning on the floor in a desperately large pool of congealing blood.

"Fuck a bucket," Zeke said. "If he dies there's no way we'll ever get to Tartarus!"

Hawke was already on his way down the spiral staircase and soon the entire team were gathered around the dying Defense Intelligence Agency official.

Kamala looked relieved. "At least we don't have to torture it out of him."

Moran's eyes flickered open. "Torture? Who the hell are you people?" His voice was hoarse and growing weaker.

"You can call us ECHO," Lexi said.

The eyes narrowed. "As in the ECHO team on the Most Wanted list?"

"Yes, but you don't get the cigar until you tell us what we want to know," Lexi said.

"No. If you save my life, I'll get you immunity."

Camacho blew out a breath and shook his head. "Sorry, but we can't do that. You tell us where Tartarus is, and we'll stop the bleeding. If you don't, you'll bleed out here on the floor. Could take hours to die and there's no one to call for help. Hell, I might even tie you up and gag you to stop you trying."

"I can't tell you where it is," he whispered. "It's worth more than my life."

Scarlet peered closer at the wound. "Your life currently has around two hours to run, so that's not saying much."

"Please…"

"There is no *'please'*," Lexi said. "Give us what we want to know, or you die. It's that simple."

Moran hesitated. Looked like he was wavering. Lexi leaned in closer and went through his pockets. Pulling out a wallet, she found what she was looking for. "Is this your wife?"

Moran nodded. "Jennifer."

"And these are your kids?"

"Yeah, Amy and Zoe. They're grown up now."

"You have a beautiful family, Mr Moran," Lexi said. "Take it from someone who has no family, that you are a very lucky man. Before today's sunset, your wife will be a widow, and your two daughters will have no father." She put the wallet gently back in his pocket and patted it. "Where is Tartarus?"

Moran's face was a storm of conflicting thoughts. Tightened brow, eyes squeezed shut, he moaned as the blood continued to stream from the wound. "All right, all right… I'll tell you, but for God's sake, don't ever tell anyone it was me who gave you the location. If you do, they'll kill the three beautiful women you just saw in that photo."

"We have a deal," Lexi said. "You have my word, Mr Moran, and I *never* go back on my word. No one will ever know you were the source."

"Okay, then," he whispered, pointing a shaking finger at Lexi. "I'll tell you, and only you. I don't know why, but I like you. I bet you don't take any shit at all."

"You win your bet." She leaned in, turning her head and positioning her ear an inch above his mouth. "Now, give me the location."

Slowly, the wounded man's lips began to move.

"I've got it." She got to her feet and looked at the others. "You won't believe where it is."

"And?" Lea said.

"There's no time left," Moran said. "Zamkov has initiated some sort of self-destruct sequence across the entire base."

"Details?" Hawke said.

"It's an ATBIP."

"ATBIP?" Kamala asked. "What's that?"

"It means Aviation Thermobaric Bomb of Increased Power," Ryan said. "A common nickname for it is the Father of all Bombs, or the Papa of all Bombs, as the

Russians like to call it. It's their equivalent of the American GBU-43/B."

"The Mother of all Bombs?" Hawke said. "Now, I've heard of *that* one."

"Right, well the MOAB has a tactical yield roughly the same as some of the smaller tactical nuclear bombs and is more than enough to turn this entire compound into ash and dust."

Moran laughed weakly. "The MOAB or even the FOAB is *nothing* compared to the Ded."

"Ded?"

"It means grandfather in Russian," Ryan said grimly.

"Fitting, no?" Moran said. "Considering it's so much more powerful than the Father of all Bombs. Zamkov truly is insane. And to think we were going to buy arms off him."

Camacho was astonished. "You were going to buy arms for the US Government from Zamkov?"

"Wait," Hawke said. ""How much more powerful is this Ded bomb than the MOABs?"

"The blast yield of the MOAB is eleven tons of TNT," Ryan said. "And the FOAB's blast yield is forty-four tons."

"Mere babies," Moran whispered. "Zamkov told me the Ded bomb has a blast yield of well over one hundred tons of TNT. Trust me when I say that after the detonation, there will be a hole in this part of the jungle visible from the Space Station."

"Where is this bomb?" Hawke said.

"On the roof of the helicopter hangar. He showed it to me earlier."

"And what about Zamkov?" Lea asked. "Where is he now?"

"He went with that goddam robot butler of his to somewhere called Lab 7G. It's to the west of the control room."

"We'll need to split again," Hawke said, turning to Eduardo. "Listen, you have to release the prisoners in the compound and then get them and your people off the mesa as fast as possible to avoid the detonation, do you understand?"

"Yes, I think so, but what about the robots?"

Hawke considered the problem. "Ryan's already deactivated many of them, right?"

Ryan nodded.

"So, Ryan, you stay here and try and shut down the rest of the AI systems. That should give Eduardo and the others a fighting chance. We also need a team to hit the lab and another to find and deactivate this grandfather bomb."

"All good," Ryan said, pointing at Moran. "But what about him?"

"He's dead," Kamala said quietly.

They looked down and saw her gently laying his head down on the concrete floor.

"Time to move out," Hawke said. "Eduardo, lead your people away off the mesa to the north. Scarlet, you do the bomb. Take Nikolai and Jack – he's the best bomb disposal expert we have. I'll take everyone else out to the labs and take Zamkov out. Good luck, everyone."

CHAPTER THIRTY-FIVE

To Nikita Zamkov, what others had dismissed as a nightmare was really a dream, and now that dream was all but over. As he watched the rockets continue to burn on the launchpads from the windows of Lab 7G, his vision of a world cleared of human detritus melted away before his very eyes. And yet, a shred of hope still existed.

Surrounded by three men and one robot, he looked down at the supervirus vial in his hand.

Eschaton.

A smile crawled over the Russian's face. Building a new race of AI robots to inhabit the world was one thing, but what was the use of that if there were nearly eight billion people to compete with for resources?

No, humanity was spent, and the supervirus his scientists had painstakingly developed here in Vyraj would be the human world's closing chapter. The invaders might have destroyed the rockets, but the burning death in his hands was still alive. There were other ways to deploy it, but it meant acting fast.

The first place to be wiped out would be Mexico City.

The Dove had a place there. Somewhere in Iztapalapa, down in the winding warrens of filth and crime to be found at the base of Molcajete Hill. It didn't matter. No one could stop the Dove; he would be untouchable.

Untouchable in the heart of a city of nearly ten million people, and a city just a few hours' drive from the United States. A city located in a country from which hundreds of thousands of illegal immigrants crossed the US southern border every year. And what if those illegal immigrants were all carrying the supervirus in their bloodstream?

And Europe nor Asia would escape the supervirus's reach, either.

Zamkov's eyes sparkled. "Yakov, tell the pilots to file four flight plans; one to Mexico City, one to Paris and one to Hong Kong. For now, the fourth is classified. Have Valentina wait for me on board the fourth jet, please." He paused and breathed a sigh of relief. "Operation Eschaton is diminished, but not dead."

"Yes, sir," said the almost-human voice. "Are we going on a vacation, sir?"

The naivety touched the Butcher's blackened heart. "You could say that, Yakov. I would like you to upgrade your program with the basic Svetovid warrior protocols."

Yakov was silent and still and his eyes went black. Five seconds later, the artificial eyes flickered back to life. "It is done, sir."

"Good. Is the Zamkov IV still intact?"

"Yes, sir."

"Order its launch."

"Yes, sir."

Now, the Butcher of Rublyovka turned to the three sombre faces of his most loyal lieutenants, and saw a fierce rage burning in all of their eyes. "You men are my greatest warriors – my greatest friends."

The three men glanced at one another, each unsure they had heard the Russian correctly when he had used the word *friends*.

Zamkov missed the moment. He had turned his back on them while picking up three small metal medical boxes. When he faced them, he was holding all three in a little tower in his arms.

"With the primary rockets destroyed, we have only the Zamkov IV now. It's much smaller and will only deliver its payload to one city – Rio de Janeiro. This will trigger an outbreak in the South American continent, but we need more, and now after the destruction we have witnessed today, there is no way to deliver the supervirus to all the intended targets. The animals who attacked us today think they have won, but they have not won. They have failed. Their only achievement was to slow us down. Instead of deploying Eschaton from the air, you will deploy it from the ground. You will be the vectors for Eschaton."

Another shared glance, more nervous this time.

"Barbosa." He handed him the first box. "You will travel to Hong Kong and deploy the vials in this box. This will be Asia's ground zero."

Barbosa said nothing as he accepted the medical box.

"Rodrigues, you will break your vials in Paris and infect the European landmass from there."

The short man from Salvador took his box with steady hands, but again said nothing.

"Finally, the Dove. You will take your vials to Mexico City and infect Latin and North America from there."

He handed him the final medical box and took a step back to the bench. Before any of them asked the obvious question, he turned. This time he was holding three injections in his hands.

Slowly, almost lovingly, he injected each man in the upper arm. "There are nearly eight billion people on this planet. When I was born just forty years ago, there were four billion. In another forty years' time there will be over ten billion. This plague must be stopped."

With the injections finished, he gave a deep sigh. "Until a few moments ago, only one person in all seven-point-seven billion people on earth was immune – me. With these injections that number is now four. As my most loyal followers, you will join me on Eschaton Base after you have deployed the supervirus."

"I don't know where that is," the Dove said.

"Neither do I," said Barbosa.

"No one does. Only Yakov, myself and Valentina."

Rodrigues cleared his throat. "Then how will we get there?"

Zamkov smiled. "Each of these medical boxes contains four vials of the supervirus. The vials are connected to a timer, which once triggered, can never be stopped. Activation of the timer will also reveal the location of Eschaton Base. From there, we will truly rule the world. Barbosa and Rodrigues – you are dismissed. Dove, I will need you and Yakov to help me here with the final preparations before we leave Vyraj."

"Yes, sir."

Zamkov watched the two men leave the lab with their medical boxes, and then turned back to Yakov and the Brazilian. "We have much to do, my friends, and very little time to do it. Soon, the enemy will be at our gates. I can already hear their guns."

CHAPTER THIRTY-SIX

Galvanized by their takeover of Mission Control and securing the location of Tartarus, the team followed Hawke and Lea back through the compound until they reached the laboratory annex in the west. With the klaxon still blaring, they jogged down a long, central corridor, riot boots squeaking on the resin screed flooring.

Gun oil and camo paint drifted on the sterile air and tired fingers wrapped around handle grips. Ammo belts rattled. Windows on either side gave a view of a series of laboratories and workbenches full of measuring cylinders, beakers, bell jars and magnetic stirrers.

A handful of scientists in white lab coats and safety goggles stopped work and caught sight of the armed special ops team pounding through their workplace. Startled, one man reached out and hit a button on the wall behind him. Instantly, yet another loud klaxon began buzzing intermittently on all sides.

"Man, those things are getting annoying," Zeke said.

"Where's the entrance to the Genesis Lab?" Hawke called out.

Lea moved in front. "This way."

Behind them, the men and women from the laboratories were streaming out into the corridor and heading for the nearest fire exit. Lexi turned, tight leather trousers reflecting the overhead strip lights. Lifting her submachine gun, she squeezed off a few rounds above their heads. "Just hurrying them along. Anyone see 7G?"

"It's over there!" Hawke called out.

Outside the lab, Hawke and his team crouched down behind a buggy parked in the concrete corridor. A robot was walking to the lab door and when he saw them, began firing from an integrated machine gun with ferocious intent. As the bullet's pinged off the robot's head and ricocheted into the darkness, Zeke could barely bring himself to say it. "That thing is *definitely* not human."

"It's one of his robots!" Lea yelled into the comms. "Can you shut it down, Ry?"

"I'm working on it," Ryan said over the comms. "In the meantime, know this – its eye strength is a thousand times greater than yours, plus it'll have heat sensitive night vision."

"It's a wonder why people don't call you Mr Good News," Lexi said.

"Give it time."

"At least this explains why we couldn't hide from it," said Kamala.

The compact machine pistol's muzzle flashed in the darkness, strobing white light as a deadly fusillade of hundreds of rounds raked over the wall behind them. The bullets embedded themselves into the bullet-proof glass with dozens of dull thuds, each one causing a tiny spider-web fracture but causing no further damage.

"It's adjusting its aim," Zeke called out.

Lexi ran a hand over her hair and blew out a deep, frightened breath. "How are you supposed to kill something you can't kill?"

"You don't kill it," Ryan replied, his voice weak in their earpieces. "You destroy it."

"It just took about a thousand high velocity rounds," Lea said. "You are not reassuring me today."

They stormed onwards. Hawke was firing on all six cylinders as he pounded through the lab, kicking pieces of broken equipment and overturned stools out of his way.

Above his head, automatic rounds tore into a line of glass-fronted cabinets and smashed them to pieces. He spun around and returned fire, punching a row of bullet holes into a gas cannister in front of more guards.

The explosion ripped through the south end of the lab, blasting everything within a fifty-foot radius to shreds and igniting flammable chemicals. Flames quickly spread up the walls and licked at the Styrofoam ceiling tiles, rapidly eating through them and making their way up inside the loft space above the lab. Another alarm went off, shriller and quieter than the warning klaxon, and then the sprinkler system activated and the entire floor was filled with high-pressure spray from water tanks on the lab's roof.

Hawke flicked the water from his hair and reloaded his MP5.

Beside him, Lea was staring at the chaos. "Well, there's no denying that this place has definitely received ECHO's full platinum package."

"You can say that again." He smacked the drum mag into the bottom of the gun and wiped more water from his face. "I wonder if Zamkov will go for a smaller package next time?"

Lexi skidded over to them through the water and smoke. "What was that about Ryan?"

"Eh?"

"I heard something about small packages."

Over the comms, they heard Ryan giving a cynical, fake laugh. "You're about as funny as a hatful of arseholes, Zhang. You know that?"

She cocked an eyebrow. "Remind me never to borrow one of your hats."

"I hate to break this up," Lea said. "But we're running out of time, guys."

They moved out, racing for the fire escape where Reaper had set up a new position. Now, the Frenchman charged toward the last few soldiers guarding the door to the Genesis Lab. Sweeping the muzzle of his weapon from side to side, he drilled them full of holes without mercy. A flashing red safe light strobed on and off above his head as he turned and called back to the others. "Allons-y!"

Inside the lab, they strained their eyes in the flashing nightmare. They found so sign of Zamkov, but there was a sealed bio-containment door at the far end of the lab.

Zeke cursed. "Son of a bitch must be somewhere – try that door!"

Reaper stormed forward and prised the door open with a crowbar. The two of them then worked together to push the thick, steel door open and they stepped inside.

"Over there!" Lea shouted. "It looks like some sort of storage container."

"Be careful," Hawke said. "All the cabinets are marked with the biohazard sign."

They stepped up to the long line of glass-fronted cabinets and saw several tiny trays containing little glass vials. "I don't like the look of that," Lea said. "Not one little bit."

"Holy Jesus on a Graham cracker," Zeke said. "Some of them are missing."

The words hit Lea like a hammer. The wise-cracking Texan was as sharp-eyed as an eagle and when he needed to be, be more serious than an undertaker. "Are you sure?"

The tall man strode past her and pointed into the corner. "There are twelve vials missing from this little tray right over here."

She moved forward, looking inside the cabinet. "Oh God, no! Whatever the hell Zamkov has been cooking up in here, he must have taken some with him before getting away!"

"Wait, let's just make sure," Kamala said.

"Yes, why don't you do that?"

The voice was robotic and cold, and when Lea turned, she almost froze with fear. Standing in between the first biosafety cabinet and the doorway was the most lifelike robot she had ever seen in her entire life. Two military robots with machineguns integrated into their arms flanked him, and then all three moved forward together.

Zeke fired on them. It was impulsive and hopeless. The bullets pinged off their titanium exoskeletons and barely caused a scratch.

"Surrender your arms," Yakov said. Either side of him, the two military robots raised their machinegun arms and aimed them at the ECHO team.

Lea took one look at the four matte black rotary cannons where their hands should be, and knew the game was up. A quick glance at Hawke told her he was thinking the same thing: we might be down, but we're not out.

"Now," Yakov repeated. "And raise your hands."

Hawke still had a gun in an ankle holster, and he prayed the robot couldn't see through his clothes to locate it. He lowered his other gun to the floor, and the others followed his lead and put their hands up.

"Now what?" Hawke asked.

"Mr Zamkov desires the pleasure of your company." Turning to the two killer robots, he said, "Escort the prisoners to Sector 9E."

Electrical pulses fired and hydraulics whined as the killer Z-bots came to life, raising the muzzles of their cannons into the prisoners' faces.

"Looks like we're going to meet Zamkov after all," Lea said.

"Yeah," Zeke said. "Lucky us."

CHAPTER THIRTY-SEVEN

Sector 9E was an auxiliary control room to the west of the labs, and when they arrived it was just in time to hear Zamkov screaming more orders at Machete and his commandos through a two-way radio. Most of them had died fighting out on the launchpads, and now the rest were engaged in a firefight defending the grandfather bomb from Scarlet up in the helicopter hangar.

Now, the Butcher turned to see what Yakov had caught back in 7G, or the Genesis Lab, as he liked to call it. "So, you are the scum that have laid waste to my beautiful creations."

Hawke returned the fake smile. "Yes, and we're available for parties and corporate events, too."

Zamkov smashed his hand down on the edge of the control console. "No! You will not mock me in this place. You will not kill my creations and make jokes."

"I think I just did," he said, goading him.

The Russian smiled and nodded. "I see what you think. You think you have beaten me, is that right?"

"It's looking that way, Nikita," Lea said. "Why not just admit defeat?"

"Because I am not defeated," he said coolly. "That is why."

Behind him, a wicked smirk grew on the face of the Dove as the Russian walked over to the center of the console. In a tense silence, his heels clicked on the smooth, hard floor. It was clear to everyone how much he relished holding court. He turned with a flourish and with a few words of soft Russian, activated the giant bank of monitors fixed to the wall above the control console. The dead screens flickered to life to reveal a rocket on the back of a truck, surrounded by a modest cloud of evaporating water.

"In less than fifteen minutes, the Zamkov IV will launch into low earth orbit."

Hawke and Lea shared a stricken glance.

"What?" Zamkov crowed. "You thought you had destroyed all the launchpads? Yes, you did, but you didn't destroy the missile truck located behind the labs." His eyes fixed on them like lasers as his face broke into a smile. "Did you?"

"Fuck you, Zamkov," Zeke said.

"I think this is checkmate," he continued.

"We destroyed the main missile attack, Zamkov," Lea said. "That's still gotta hurt."

"More than you could ever know," he said. "The main attack was a thing of beauty. Three multistage rockets all blasting into their new home five hundred miles above the earth, and then manoeuvring until in the correct place to release their payloads."

Lea stared at the truck-mounted rocket in horror. "The biohazard cabinet we found in the lab! You've created some sort of virus!"

"Yes, or more precisely," Zamkov continued, "ten separate vials of the most deadly supervirus every created, each one carefully developed with unique pathogens found here in the cave system inside this tepui. Along with the pristine bacteria to be found here, there are in these caves a lot of other nasties totally unknown to the outside world. Using them, I have created something totally unique, with a killing power stronger than Ebola and with the vectors of the common cold. Quite delicious, and quite devastating to humanity."

"And don't tell me," Lea said, "you tested the supervirus out on your slaves as well?"

"This is the only way to get such accurate results. We are talking about something of pure beauty, and until you arrived, it would have been delivered to the most populous city of every continent via a system of multiple, independently targetable re-entry vehicles."

"Designed by you," she said with disgust.

He gave a mock bow. "Designed by me, and because I designed the software running the American, Russian and Chinese early warning systems, it was safe to say the supervirus bombs would have reached their destinations."

"Sorry to throw a spanner in your works," Hawke said.

Zamkov ignored him. "Tokyo in Japan, Shanghai in China, Jakarta in Indonesia, Mumbai in India, Lagos in Nigeria, Mexico City in Mexico, Moscow in Russia, London in the United Kingdom, New York City in the USA and São Paulo right here in Brazil… all would have been full of millions of infected people."

"*Would* have been," Kamala said. "Too bad we screwed that up for you."

"You have only slowed me down. It can still be deployed, and I designed a full month-long incubation period to maximize the number of people who are infected before the symptoms become obvious. Then there will be panic, but as they flee the cities, they will infect even more people living in the countryside."

"Hell on earth," Scarlet said.

"Heaven, actually." Zamkov turned from the fuelling rocket back to his prisoners. "Imagine a world with a population of billions, but instead of those billions being filthy, rude, incompetent humans busily consuming the planet's resources, they would be billions of clean, polite, efficient AI machines, reducing the planet's carbon emissions and consuming practically no resources at all. You should thank me. I'm saving the planet."

"And getting a world of slaves into the bargain?" Lea said. "I don't think so."

"Who said anything about slaves? Robots are not slaves, at least not my AI creations. The world I envisage would be made of billions of AI robots just like Yakov here; calm, in control of themselves, and entirely autonomous."

"You'd have no control over them at all?" Lea said. "Sounds like trouble to me. What if they got it into their heads to tear their glorious creator limb from limb one day?"

Zamkov furrowed his brow. "This could never happen, there are fail-safes. I have an override switch."

"So if there's any trouble with your population, you can just shut it down?" Lea said. "Sounds just like slaves to me."

"No!" he snapped. "They are not slaves. They are my creations. I love them – every single one of them, and once my AI armies have buried the dead, the entire planet will be a blank slate, simply waiting for me to redesign a smarter, cleaner, safer world."

Kamala lowered her voice and leaned closer to Zeke. "This isn't insane at all."

"You can say that again."

Lea said, "Makes the Oracle seem level and balanced… almost."

"And all that ruined by *us*," Hawke said. "What a crying shame."

"Yes, you hurt me, but you have not destroyed Eschaton. Many have tried and failed. All things considered, you have had no more success in bringing me down than the local tribes. A few well-placed holograms kept them at bay, but you have required a firmer hand."

"Wait," Lea said, recalling the beast with the fiery eyes she had seen out in the jungle. "*That's* what the monster was? A hologram?"

Zamkov smiled. "Ah – so you have met one of the jungle spirits? I'm very proud of them. The projection technology is incorporated at various places in the jungle surrounding the mesa and the tepui itself."

"That's impossible," Lea said. "Creating 3D holograms requires bounce screens and mylar and god knows what else."

Hawke looked at her and she shrugged. "First husband."

"Got it."

"Yes, you are right – in 2019," Zamkov said. "You're forgetting how far ahead my technology is. If humanity wasn't about to end, it would take another twenty years to develop this level of holographic technology."

"We're not going to let you get away with this," Lea said.

Zamkov chuckled. "What can you do? We still have the truck-launched Zamkov IV – you might have seen us test one earlier. It made low earth orbit. That alone will ensure the supervirus infects millions of people in Rio de Janeiro and the surrounding state."

"It can be contained in South America," Lea said. "We'll contact the authorities and have all flights and ships quarantined."

Zamkov laughed again, a deep cynical growl. "You think I am so stupid that I would leave the fate of the world in the hands of one rocket? I also have three of my most loyal warriors personally delivering more vials of the supervirus to classified locations around the world. No, my friends, you have not ended Eschaton. You have merely slowed it down. Now, if you will excuse me, I have a flight to catch."

"You're never going to get away with this, Zamkov!" Lea called out.

He turned and summoned Yakov and the Dove. "I already have *got away with it*," he said with a snarl. "You, on the other hand, are about to find out what it feels like to be shot by four rotary cannons firing seven thousand rounds per minute. The last men I tested these guns on looked like dog food in less than sixty seconds."

Hawke moved toward Zamkov, but surprised everyone by sidestepping the Russian and tackling the Dove. Spinning around, his elbow bone hit the Brazilian in the center of his face. A solid, no-nonsense strike that split the nose bone down the middle and sent a thin mist of blood bursting out between them. The Brazilian man didn't make a sound or take a step back.

As Hawke squared up to him for a second swing, the Dove spun around on his hip and hooked his legs out from under him. Hawke tumbled over, crashing down on the smooth tiled floor and instantly rolling to his left to avoid the Dove's next blow.

Hawke pulled his gun, but the Brazilian kicked out and knocked it from his hands. It clattered on the floor and the robots moved to fire on the Englishman, but the Russian raised his hands. "No! Let them fight!"

Scrambling on the floor, Hawke reached for the weapon with outstretched fingers, but the Dove swung his boot into the Englishman's face and knocked him on his back. Blood leaked out from a long cut on Hawke's cheek and his head was spinning like a superbike's rear wheel. Trying to bring his eyes back into focus, the klaxon still barking above his head, his next clear vision was of the Dove picking up the gun and pointing at him.

"You should have killed me when you had the chance."

Hawke said nothing. The Dove lifted the barrel higher, changing the aim from his chest to his bleeding face. Hawke staggered up to his knees. He wiped the blood from the deep cut on his cheek and fixed his attention not on the gun, but on the Brazilian's mud-brown eyes.

"I still *do* have the chance."

The smile faded. "What are you talking about?"

Hawke looked at the man intently. Even through the black, bloodshot eye and the fat, swollen lip, it was possible to see the real man, the man behind the mask. Those eyes told a story of pain and suffering and rage, but this man had channelled that anger into the wrong place.

"The Glock's out of rounds."

"You're bluffing."

"Why not pop the mag out and look for yourself?"

"You think I'm stupid?"

Again, Hawke said nothing. He was weighing his options. He was a highly trained commando and Special Forces operative. He knew how to count, and he knew there was still one more round sitting in the chamber of the gun in the Dove's hand. He also knew the extractor was sitting just outside the slide.

Hard to see. Impossible if you didn't know what you were looking for, but it meant there was a bullet sitting right there in the chamber. The doubt on the Dove's face told him he was unaware of how to read the Glock's chamber indicator.

Keep him busy.

"I never said you were stupid."

"All I have to do is pull the trigger, and we will see who is right."

Hawke said, "And all you'll get is a dry click, and then we go again. Think you can win?"

"I don't need to fight you, Englishman," he snarled, and thumbed back the matte black hammer at the back of the gun. "Say your prayers."

CHAPTER THIRTY-EIGHT

Still kneeling, Hawke unleashed his rolled fist and drove a shovel hook up through the air. It was a brutal, savage strike, coming at the Dove from an oblique angle of forty-five degrees and making contact with his lower jaw at a terrifying rate of speed.

The jawbone snapped and several teeth shattered. His head clicked back like the lid on a silver cigarette lighter. The muscle-packed Brazilian fell back and crashed onto the floor with a heavy, organic thud with the gun still in his hand and then everything was still.

Hawke knew he was still alive. He hadn't hit him that hard, and he could see the man's ribcage expanding and contracting as he breathed through his unconsciousness. He unfurled the man's fingers and took back possession of the Glock. Hefting the sidearm in his hand, this was no weapon for a fool. No safety catch, for one thing. Checking the gun, a bleak smile danced on his lips. He'd been right. One bullet sitting right there in the chamber, but it still felt like a pyrrhic victory, unless... As Zamkov ordered Yakov to pick the Dove up, Hawke moved on the Russian.

Instantly, the killer robots whirred into action, their metallic skulls and red eyes swivelling on him and the cannons in their arms pointing in his face. Taking no chances, Zamkov gave Yakov new orders to leave the Dove and aim another gun at the prisoners.

The Butcher of Moscow watched in dark satisfaction as Yakov trained the Veresk submachine gun on the captives. It looked like he had taken to his new programming even better than expected. "Lie very still," Zamkov said. "Or he will annihilate every last one of you. He is running my latest AI killer robot fusion software on his neural network. He will not discriminate, and he will not hesitate. His cognitive and physical reactions are thousands of times faster than yours. Aren't they, Yakov?"

"Yes, sir."

"Fucking hell, Joe," Lea said. "We're being held prisoner by a mannequin."

"Please," Hawke said, hands crossed on the back of his head, "you're making me feel like a real dummy."

He heard Lea groan. "We're about to get killed by the Terminator and you're making jokes."

"Yes, you are about to get killed," Zamkov said.

"Never gonna happen, bud," Hawke said, making his move. He drew a combat knife from his belt holster, lunged forward, gripped the Russian's wrist and pulled him across his body. "I'm no computer nerd, but my good friend who is, told me that these machines will have been programmed not to kill you, am I right?"

"Of course, I am their creator."

"So, as long as your body is between me and RoboCop over there, I'm doing all right."

"If you say so," the Russian said.

"Order it to drop the gun and shut itself down, or I'll push this blade through your jugular right now. You know what a jugular does, right?"

Zamkov struggled in the former commando's grip, a sweat beginning to bead on his forehead for the first time. "Of course."

"Then do it." Hawke pushed the tip of the blade into his throat. "Not much wiggle room left now, Butcher. Any further, and this steel will be in your veins."

"Stop! Stop, please. I will do as you ask."

Lea and the others looked on, their eyes jumping nervously between the robot and its master, who was still struggling in Hawke's grip.

"Now, Zamkov!" Hawke's voice boomed in the control room.

"Yakov, please drop the weapon and go to sleep."

The gun clattered to the floor.

"Not sleep," Ryan called out over the comms. "He needs to shut down, not go to sleep."

"You heard the man," Hawke said, scraping the tip of the blade across his skin and repositioning it just under his jawline. "Shut the fucking thing down, and anymore tricks and you die first."

"Yakov, please shut yourself down… *totally*."

"I comply."

The robot's eyes went black and its head slumped forward. Still and silent, it stood on the spot like a frozen sentry.

Zamkov stared at his creation with sad, desperate eyes. "There."

"Now shut the other two down," Hawke said.

The Russian obeyed and the two Z-bots powered down. "What happens now?"

"What do you think?" Lea said.

"You have destroyed Vyraj, blown up my rockets, neutralized the supervirus threat and deactivated my AI systems. What is left for you to do? Kill me?"

"We don't murder people in cold blood," Lea said.

"You cannot arrest me," he crowed, feeling braver now. "You cannot report me to the Brazilian authorities or any other government – those I don't own and control are dependent on my systems to run their countries. You cannot touch me."

"That's not strictly true though, is it?" Lea said.

"What do you mean?"

Lea paused a beat and studied his face. Sooke's and Ryan's research had raised the spectre of a murder lurking in Zamkov's past, and now was the time to confront him about it. "Remember Valentina Kiriyenko?"

Zamkov's eyes narrowed. He looked like he had seen a ghost, or at least, heard the name of one. "What did you just say?"

"Valentina Kiriyenko," Lea repeated. "You raped and murdered her at university and used your money to get away with the crime."

"What are you talking about?" he sneered.

"You know what I'm talking about. We might be fugitives but we're not without friends, and some of those friends have other friends… in low places. When we had your name, we asked them to look into you."

"And so you found out about the woman," he growled. "So what?"

"You know who she was, right?"

He backed down. His voice grew quieter. "Of course."

"I thought you might. She was the daughter of Boris Kiriyenko. You remember Mr Kiriyenko, don't you?"

"Yes."

"I thought you might remember him, too. Boris Kiriyenko is the head of one of the biggest organized crime networks in Russia. The criminal empire he controls is vast, and the FBI not only list him as one of the most dangerous men on the planet, but they also have him on their Most Wanted list."

"Yes," Lexi purred. "Three places below us."

Zamkov was growing more nervous by the second. "What are you getting at?"

"Up to now, Boris Kiriyenko has racked up quite the charge sheet – money laundering, tax evasion, kidnapping and there's even some dark rumors of murdering rival gang bosses."

Suddenly, everything had changed for Zamkov. "Please…"

"Thing is, Butcherman, we know the sort of people who can track Mr Kiriyenko down, and when he finds out we can give him the man who murdered his little girl, I'm positive we can make a deal with him. He gives us some money, and we give him you. The last person he killed was one of his thugs. He stole a few thousand bucks from him during a blackmailing shakedown." Lea's voice grew lower as she walked over to him, almost face to face. "They took him out to a dacha and made his death last three hours. Not to get into too much detail, but they didn't have to buy pigfeed for a few days. Just imagine what he'll do to the man who did *that* to his daughter."

"But you would have to be *alive* to do the things you talk about," Zamkov purred, and without pause he yelled at Yakov. "Override Omega 35!"

Yakov instantly reactivated and whirred into action, rounding on Hawke and raising his gun. Aiming precisely at the Englishman, Zamkov stopped him at the last minute and gave the two other robots the same command. "The kill decision rests with all my creations, but I just gave them the code overriding the protocol not to kill me. It's in their minds now, in their own internal neural networks. They are ready to kill you now, even if it means killing me. What's it going to be? You want your team torn to pieces, just so you can know I am dead for the few seconds you have before your own deaths?"

Hawke sighed and released the Russian. "You win." His words were punctuated by a ground-shaking explosion, and then seconds later, Scarlet's voice over the comms. "We just took out a missile truck, Joe. Looks like he was about to launch from there too."

Zamkov's face turned red as the rage rose on his heart. "No! No, no, no! You cannot do this to me!" Behind him, a dazed, bruised and bleeding Dove staggered to his feet.

Lea smiled. "Already done, Zamkov."

The Russian fought to control himself. "I still have my warriors! I still have my lieutenants. They will never let me down."

"We'll get them, too."

Zamkov laughed. "Two have already flown away like macaws, my friends."

Lea and Hawke braced when they heard the news. Maybe, she thought, he's bluffing?

"So you see, there's no way out of this," Zamkov said. "Kiriyenko will never find me, and this whole place is rigged with the most powerful conventional bomb ever developed."

"Then you will die too," Lea said.

He shrugged. "Better to die here in a split second than after hours of torture in Kiriyenko's dacha. Goodbye, and good death." He stopped dead, then pointed at Kamala. "And bring her with us, Yakov – she is our insurance policy. Come after me and Yakov here will put a bullet through her brain."

"No!" Lea yelled. "Take me, not her."

Zamkov laughed wildly, then, as he, Yakov and the Dove stepped out of the lab, dragging Kamala behind them, he paused and spoke to the robots. "Wait until we're in the elevator and then kill them."

The door shut and Hawke watched Zamkov approach the elevator. The robots were watching too, via cameras in the backs of the heads.

"What the hell are we going to do, chief?" Zeke asked. "We can't rush them, and we can't shoot at them!"

"They're going to rip us to shreds, Joe!"

When the elevator doors slid shut, the robots raised their cannons into the aim and opened fire.

CHAPTER THIRTY-NINE

They dived for cover behind the console, and the robots let rip, drilling bullet holes all over it and the back wall without mercy. Seeing their targets had taken cover, they coordinated with each other and each took one end of the long control console. Finding them taking cover behind it, they raised their arms and prepared to fire once again.

Lea gasped. "Holy shit, Joe! This is really it!"

And then the attack stopped. The robots stopped moving and their arms dropped uselessly at the sides of their exoskeletons. Slowly, the red lights in their eye sockets grew dimmer and then faded out completely.

Ryan's voice crackled over the comms. "I think I might have worked out how to hack the AI master control and shut the rest of the robots down."

"You think?!" Lea said. "Fuck me, I love you, Ryan!"

Hawke raised an eyebrow. "Steady on."

"You did it, Ryan, my boy!" Zeke said. "I'm buying you a goddam crate of beer when we get outta here, man."

"I take it I was just in time?"

"Er, yeah mate," Hawke said. "You could say that. Any word from Cairo?"

"She's still fighting her way up to the hanger. Machete's giving them hell."

"We're on our way but we have to get Zamkov first. He's got Kamala. You get up to Cairo's position ASAP."

"On my way."

Hawke led the reunited ECHO team up to the lab roof where they scanned the compound for any sign of Zamkov. Any hope in their hearts was crushed to dust when they heard the sound of twin engines roaring behind an ATC tower north of the lab. When they saw a black and silver Sukhoi Business Jet powering up into the humid Amazon air, they lowered their guns and breathed a collective sigh of regret.

"We lost him."

Lea looked into the sky, almost dark now. The Sukhoi's navigation lights flashed in the jungle twilight as the gear retracted. Then they saw a second jet, even further away to the north. "Jesus Christ – didn't he say his most loyal warriors had extra vials of the supervirus?"

"Sure did," Zeke said. "And that two of them had already flown the nest, too. If you ask me, Mr Doveman was the third bird, flying out of here ahead of Zamkov, and the Butcher himself is on that last damned Sukhoi."

They heard screams over the comms and were shocked back into action. "This isn't over," Hawke said. "Cairo needs us."

They sprinted across to the hangar along the monorail. Below them, Ryan was approaching on the ground and they converged at the base of a concrete ramp leading up to the helicopter hangar. When they got to the top, Hawke saw Scarlet up ahead. She was walking toward him with her gun over her shoulder.

"I take it Machete is…" he asked.

She tipped her head. "He's having a lie down."

"Great work, Cairo. I suppose the rest of his platoon are just as sleepy?"

"All dead," she said without emotion. "They fought like tigers though, especially Carneiro. In another universe he could have been on the team."

"In another universe," Lea repeated.

"Zamkov?" Scarlet asked.

"Flew away, along with the Dove," Lea said. "I'm sorry, Cairo. We did all we could."

"Wait," the former SAS captain said. "Where's Kamala."

Lea broke the news. "And we also have reason to believe there are others working for Zamkov. We think there are three of them, all equipped with vials of the supervirus."

"Christ on a unicycle," Scarlet said. "You let them go?"

"We had no choice!" the Irishwoman snapped back.

"There's no time for that," Hawke said. "We have to neutralize the grandfather bomb before it detonates and blows us all sky high. With luck, Eduardo will have got the prisoners well away by now, but we're well and truly in the thick of it."

"It's up one more level," Scarlet said.

Reaching the top of the ramp, they emerged into a vast space, most of which was undercover except for an area of rolled-back roofing over the helipad. From the very highest point of the compound, the views across the jungle were even more breathtaking, especially at this late time of the day. In the distance, white-water floodplains shimmered in a heat haze.

"So, where's grandpa?" Scarlet said.

"My best guess would be over there," Lea said, pointing behind her friend.

Scarlet turned. "Ah."

In the corner of the hanger was a fifty-foot long missile-shaped bomb tethered to a stainless-steel trailer, painted black and with Z1 stencilled on the side in white. Beside the designation was the Russian word for grandfather, written in Zamkov's language: Дед.

Lexi looked at Scarlet and asked deadpan, "You think that might be it?"

"Piss off, Zhang. I was looking in the other direction."

"Of course you were." Lexi winked. "Glad it wasn't more armed soldiers over there, in that case."

Scarlet squared up to her and curled her hand into a fist. "You want a knuckle sandwich?"

"Oh yeah? I thought a posh girl like you would call it a knuckle baguette."

"Woah," Ryan said. "The testosterone's really pumping in here today."

Both women turned to him. Scarlet said, "Not in you, it isn't."

A howl of laughter, but Hawke broke up the fight and pushed through the gathering to get a better look at Zamkov's parting gift. It was an awesome sight. Sleek, metallic paint shone in the hangar's strip lights and a small control panel near its tailfins showed a red digital readout.

"He wasn't bluffing," he said. "That thing's already counting down."

"He was prepared to blow up this whole place," Lea said.

Camacho took one look at the timer system and shook his head. "This ain't gonna happen, guys. I could disarm this but not in less than an hour, and I'd need a whole bunch of specialist tools as well. I guess we could raid their workshops here in the hangar…" he blew out a breath and gave his head another slow shake. "Not gonna happen. We need to get out of here and in a hurry."

"How long have we got?" Lea asked.

"Fifty-six minutes until this entire compound is nothing but a hole in the ground."

"We've disarmed a lot of bombs, Jack," Scarlet said. "Remember the cobalt bomb in San Francisco? Or on the Mount of Moses during the Atlantis mission? What makes this one so different?"

Camacho raised his eyebrows. "In a word, Zamkov."

"Exactly," Ryan said. "Or more specifically, his AI genius. This entire weapon is more than just a bomb. It's a sentient thing, it thinks, it considers. It's thinking right now, just like we are. It's identified us as a threat and it's taking defensive measures – look."

Lea leaned closer to the timer. "Is that thing getting faster?"

"It is," Ryan said. "It's running ten seconds down in around eight seconds, and by the looks of things, the rate is increasing. If we try and tamper with it, my money is on the damn thing blowing up right now."

"I'm not happy working on it," Camacho said. "This mother is going off in less than an hour and we'd better be at least five miles away from this mesa, or we're dead."

"We can do that," Zeke said. "Right?"

"What, get across the compound, down the mesa and do five miles of jungle in less than an hour?" Nikolai asked. "I don't think so."

"Ideas?" Hawke said.

"There has to be a chopper around here somewhere," Zeke said.

Lea shook her head. "Zamkov ordered all the spare choppers and planes to be destroyed."

"Hold on," Scarlet said. "I saw some paramotors over up on a rooftop helipad just to the west of this hangar."

Hawke hoped she was right. "I guess Zamkov used them for hunting people, but it sounds like it's our only chance."

"Then let's do it," Lea said. "Or we're toast."

CHAPTER FORTY

Hawke and Reaper covered everyone as they sprinted over to the helipad and climbed into Zamkov's paramotors. Hawke knew from experience he could get well over two hundred miles out of one so long as the tank was full – and they all were. That sort of range would be enough for them to get to the Japurá river in the north. There was an Eco Lodge there.

"Everyone on the comms?" he said.

One by one, everyone on the team called in. Lexi was last. "Don't forget about me."

"We won't," Hawke said. "And everyone go as fast as you can. If Zamkov wasn't bluffing about his Ded bomb, we're still well inside the blast range."

"But he's already well out of range," Lea said. "Look!"

Hawke had already seen it – the Sukhoi was receding toward the northern horizon, now no more than a tiny black insect hovering above the jungle canopy. "We'll get him," he said through gritted teeth. "And Kamala, too. All right, let's go people."

Hawke led the way, firing up the paramotor engine and then sprinting across the rooftop until the wing billowed behind him. Then he was over the edge and increasing the throttle to gain altitude. One by one they followed, and then they were leaving Vyraj behind and sailing out across the jungle. Below them, running out across the wetlands at the base of the mesa, he saw Eduardo and Paulo leading the starving, cave-dwellers out into the light. They had an hour to get away, and he knew they would probably take cover in the caves until after the blast.

"They'll be fine," he said over the comms. "And so will we."

An hour into their journey, the sky at their backs lit up. First white, then orange, and then the deep, bass roar of the grandfather bomb's explosion ripped through the twilight sky like something from their worst nightmares. Below, they watched the shockwave blasting the tops of the canopy, and sending startled birds flapping into the air.

But it was over, and everyone was safe.

Everyone except Kamala.

*

The paramotors ran out of fuel at sunset. As the sun sank into a ruby ribbon off to their left, Lea took one last look at the sky, then steered the wing to starboard. She wheeled in the sky like an eagle, and then lined up for the landing on the riverbank. Below, she saw Camacho and Scarlet had already touched down and were gathering up the enormous nylon wings into their arms by the side of the wild, clean river.

The Japurá Eco Lodge was over two hundred miles north of the Vyraj compound, nestled among the rainforest on the banks of the Japurá river, one of the many tributaries leading into the Amazon River. It was safe, and comfortable, and had showers, but none of this was enough to calm Hawke's soul.

An hour after touching down, he joined the others outside around a campfire. He took a long pull on a cold beer, and stared up at the stars as they began to prick the vast Amazon sky. With Zamkov and the supervirus on the loose, and Kamala as his hostage, Hawke couldn't relax, but he found the cold beer helped him to decompress as he planned what to do next. He sat down on a log and took another sip of his beer. They had destroyed Vyraj but Zamkov had evaded them, and taken a hostage, too. He felt a headache radiating behind his eyes. Maybe the beer wasn't such a good idea.

Moran, at least, had given up the location to Tartarus – a small artificial island tucked away at the far end of the Aleutian Islands, south of Alaska. The word 'remote' didn't do the place justice, plus there were the terrain and climate to consider. At this time of year, the place was likely to be a whiteout.

It didn't matter, he told himself. Nothing would stop them rescuing Alex, Brandon and President Brooke. Looking down into his bag at his feet, he saw the bottle of elixir he had taken from the Citadel. Thinking about getting it to Alex and helping her walk again brought a smile to his lips.

He heard Lea stepping out of the lodge and gave her a smile. He didn't get one back. Instead, she sat beside him, and explained to the team what she and Orlando Sooke had just spent the last thirty minutes discussing.

It wasn't good news.

Zamkov wasn't bluffing. Four jets had been tracked leaving the compound by Titanfort's colossal surveillance network. All short-range Sukhoi business jets, they had all landed at hubs for refuelling, but one had stayed in Mexico City. Chatter picked up by Ezra Haven suggested it would be the first place to be struck and the attack was imminent.

Scarlet shrugged her jacket off and threw it over the log. Humidity like this was shirt-only weather, but the jacket was necessary in a battle. Somewhere to stuff unspent bullets and padded leather to protect her elbows when she was rolling out of harm's way. As the team began to wind down, Ryan swatted at something on his neck.

"Wait – have we even been inoculated?" he said. "I mean this place will be swarming with yellow fever, malaria, dengue, zika… hell, there's a good chance I'll catch chikungunya."

"There's an even better chance I'll slap you upside the head," Lexi said, scowling.

"So, what are we going to do next?" Zeke asked. "I know I'm the new guy, but seems to me we can't let that son of a bitch take Kamala, right?"

Hawke lowered his head and shut his eyes. "I know."

"But what about Alex?" Ryan said.

"You heard what Sooke said! Zamkov's attack on Mexico City is imminent, Ry – within the next forty-eight hours!"

"Being in ECHO means making tough choices," Hawke said. "We can still save Alex and her father, but we can't let Zamkov kill millions of people."

"Why not just contact the Mexican Government?" Zeke asked.

"Because it would expose our location," Hawke said. "And even if we found a way around that, Zamkov still has Kamala. If the Mexican authorities deal with the Zamkov threat, there's a chance it might lead them to Zamkov. If that happens, they'll rescue her and hand her over to the Americans. I don't even want to think about what Faulkner will do to her to get vital information about us."

"Joe's right," Lea said. "We have to handle this ourselves and we have to work faster than we've ever worked before. We have to get in, find the vials, take Zamkov out and then get out again. We can't waste any time when it comes to rescuing Alex, Brandon and President Brooke."

"Agreed," Lexi said.

Reaper grumbled assent.

"We have to be careful here," Lea said. "Zamkov took Kamala as an insurance policy – something to barter with if we track him down before he can detonate the vials. He's betting on us rolling over."

"Then he's going to lose that bet," Zeke said.

"And his life," Reaper growled.

After a tense silence, Hawke finished his beer and stood up. Swatting a mosquito away, he took one last look at the stars. "Get some sleep everyone. Tomorrow, we fly to Mexico."

CHAPTER FORTY-ONE

The door smashed open and soldiers rushed into the cell. Jack Brooke barely knew what was happening before their hands were all over him and dragging him off the pull-out bed and onto the floor. One of them grabbed his arms and tried to pull them behind his back to cuff him. He resisted. Pushing out against the pressure, he got an army boot in his right-hand side.

"Don't make trouble," one of the men grunted, and reached out for his hands again.

Brooke wriggled free, spun over onto his side and kicked out, but this time the payback was with a higher rate of interest. Two soldiers piled in, kicking him hard in his midriff, while a third man finally wrestled his hands into place and slapped the cuffs on him.

"Shoulda listened to me, Brooke."

He said nothing. He was still gasping for air from the beating in his stomach.

They hefted him to his feet like a sack of potatoes, then dragged him out of the cell and into the bright lights of the corridor. He blinked, blinded by the lights. He struggled to remember how long he had been in the solitary confinement cell, but he knew he was glad to be out of it.

"It's great to be back in the real world again, assholes," he said.

"You wouldn't say that if you knew why the colonel ordered us to get you out."

Fear stung his heart. He knew Blanchard understood there was never any hope of him doing what he wanted and confessing. Even under torture, Brooke would rather die than confess to something he hadn't done, but he had an Achilles heel, and both he and the base commander knew it.

Alex.

Reaching Blanchard's office, the men knocked on the door and waited. When the colonel told them to enter, they opened the door and dragged the prisoner into the room.

"Prisoner 7832G, as you ordered, sir."

Blanchard was writing, and he continued writing without looking up. Taking his time, Brooke thought, to put me in my place. Dot every I and cross every T and make the condemned man sweat it out a bit longer, yes sir.

"You men are dismissed."

"Sir, yes sir!"

The soldiers snapped to attention and marched out of the room.

Blanchard finished his paperwork and then raised his eyes to Brooke. "Won't you have seat, Jack?"

"I know why I'm here."

"Oh, you do, huh?"

"You want me to confess to treason and implicate other loyal members of my administration, or you're going to hurt my daughter."

Blanchard twirled the pen around his fingers. "Is that what you want to happen?"

Brooke's voice grew brittle. "If you touch her, Colonel Blanchard, I will personally kill you."

Blanchard grinned. "I couldn't have heard that right, because I'm sure a man of your intelligence wouldn't have made such a threat. Would he?"

"Leave her alone, colonel."

"Then sign the confession – oh, and we'll want a video confession, too. For the media."

"I can't do that."

A long pause while Blanchard made a big deal about sighing and leaning back in his chair.

"All I have to do is pick up this phone, have my soldiers bring Alex out of her solitary confinement cell, and take her right across to Mr Mahoe's office. You remember him, right? I introduced you to him after your little escape attempt."

Brooke knew his world was imploding around him. There was no way he could do what this bastard was asking, but he couldn't let him hurt Alex, either. And yet, there was no way out of this hell, and no one in the world knew where they were.

"Well? Last chance."

Brooke's mind spun with random memories. His duty to the American people blurred together with Alex's childhood Christmases. Maintaining his presidential oath mixed with the day he dropped Alex off at college. It hurt so much, he had to fight back the pain.

Gotta keep it together, Jack.

"I won't lie to the people about committing treason."

"Then Alex goes to Mahoe." Blanchard picked up the phone, the regret in his voice almost sincere. "This is Blanchard, have Alex taken over to Mahoe."

"No!" Brooke yelled. "You rescind that order, Colonel Blanchard! I am the lawful, constitutional President of the United States and I am ordering you to stop this!"

"Sir, with all due respect, you are not. You are a prisoner of the United States Government, by order of the legal President, and this shit is happening because you won't confess."

Blanchard buzzed the soldiers back into the room. "Bring him with me."

Brooke's eyes narrowed in confusion. "Bring me where?"

The colonel turned. "You're going to watch Mahoe work on your daughter."

"No!"

But his screams were silenced by a hefty punch in the gut, and then they were dragging him down the long, concrete corridor on the way to the worst hell he could imagine.

*

Pegasus wasn't anything like Cougar had imagined. He had an annoying phone voice, and she had pictured an overweight, stuffed shirt with coffee-stained teeth. A pen-pusher with his hand in a bag of doughnuts. In reality, Tony Garcetti looked trim and tidy as he walked into the diner and slid down onto the red vinyl seat opposite her.

"Agent Cougar."

"Hey, Garcetti."

He picked up a laminated menu. Peered over the top of it and returned her gaze. "What?"

"Nothing."

"Like what you see?"

"I've seen better menus."

He pushed out a polite laugh. "We have more information."

Cougar lowered her sunglasses back over her eyes, leaned back in her seat and watched the people walking along South Figueroa Street, hands in pockets, laughing, talking in the southern Californian sunshine. "You know where ECHO are?"

"No."

"Then, what?"

"We know where they're *going* to be."

She shrugged. "I'll take that."

"Our listening station in Caracas heard about a very large explosion in the Amazon jungle and it caught their attention. They looked into it, re-tasked a few satellites, and found all sorts of interesting things. Thanks to a mole in the Titanfort surveillance hub, we tracked them down to an ecolodge in the Amazon. Can you believe that?"

"Huh."

"So, anyway, it turns out they're on their way to Mexico City."

"Why?"

"We don't know. It doesn't matter. The important thing is that they'll be touching down at Mexico City International Airport within the next twenty-four hours and you're going to be there when that happens. Your orders remain the same, Cougar – the entire team is to be neutralized, just the same way you dealt with the first three."

"Leave it to me."

"And then what?"

She hadn't heard the question. She was watching a couple argue out on the street. She thought about stepping in and handling it, but then they kissed and made up. Walked on. She turned back to Garcetti and saw a question on his face. "You say something?"

"I asked what your plan is after the contract is finished."

"Why do you want to know?"

"Just shooting the breeze."

"A man like you doesn't shoot the goddam breeze, Garcetti."

He laughed. This time it was more authentic. "I guess not."

"I'm getting out of here, if you must know. No more jobs. No more killing."

He mulled the words over, appreciating every ounce of the sentence as if he was tasting a fine red wine. “You think you can do that?”

“Why not?”

He shrugged. “In my experience, former – how shall I put it? Former *government workers* can’t just fold up their baggage like a suitcase. The work you do weighs too much.”

“What are you, my mother?”

“I’m just saying, be realistic.” He slid a card across the table. “This is my personal number, Jessica. When I walk out of here, we won’t meet or talk again, but if you ever need any help from the inside… well, you can call me.”

CHAPTER FORTY-TWO

Breakfast was served on the deck with the sun rising over the river. Already well over thirty degrees Celsius before dawn, the morning was like every other here, hot and humid. A sultry breeze shuffled across the water from the south bank of the Japurá, the air already teeming with flying insects.

Less agile were the ECHO team. After the battle on the mesa, their bones ached, and their skin was cut and bruised. Worse, the kidnapping of their newest member, Kamala Banks, had plunged them all into the darkest of places. The long list of ECHO members slaughtered in the course of the team's missions was a stark reminder that she might already be dead, but no one would accept that until they knew for sure.

In the background, the lodge's 110v generator hummed gently. When the noise quietened for a few seconds, the lights above their head dimmed, then back to their full brightness as the generator picked up. Hawke had been silent a long time. He was resting a cup of coffee on his knee, staring through the mosquito screen at the river.

A young couple, German maybe, or Swedish, were making their way down river in one of the lodge's wooden canoes. He was paddling in the rear and she was snapping photographs as a cloud of parakeets burst into the air above the trees and squawked away into the sunrise. Behind them, a *peke-peke* or motorized canoe, waş pootling in the other direction with some older people on board. Ahead of them, just beyond the lodge's private beach, came the sound of howling and whooping from the Monkey Sanctuary.

Scarlet looked at Ryan, but resisted making a joke she had considered about his family coming to see him. No one was in the mood. And, he had never spoken about his family. For all she knew, he had none, and that meant a very unfunny joke. Instead, she drank some freshly squeezed mango juice and perused the plates of untouched breakfast on the table in front of her; she wasn't in the mood for that, either.

Lea spoke first. "We all know we've got a big mother of a problem, and we all slept on that problem, right?"

Ryan yawned. "Speak for yourself. Those insects were *raging* last night."

She ignored it. "We all know it's up to us to rescue Alex, President Brooke and Brandon, but we also have a duty to stop Zamkov and get Kamala back."

"Agreed." It was the first thing Hawke had said all morning. "I'm not leaving anyone in this team behind, not ever. We owe her everything and we have to get her back."

"That's presuming she's…" Ryan stopped speaking and put his sunglasses on. "Sorry."

Hawke gave him a look. "We all knew what we were doing when we signed up to this life. We risk everything every day and sometimes, it's all for nothing. This wasn't one of those times. We needed the location of Tartarus and we got it, and more than that, we shut down Zamkov's insane Roboland. Yes, the plan was to go straight to Tartarus, but now we have to change that plan. We can't let the Butcher spread the supervirus in Mexico City, and we can't just abandon Kamala. Only then can we get our lives back and live with ourselves at the same time."

"Sure, when we get our lives back." The emotion rose in Lea's usually calm voice. "When we get Faulkner out of the Oval Office, when we get President Brooke back into power, and when we get our names off the Most Wanted. Then we can go home, at last."

"And where is home for you guys?" Zeke asked.

"We have a place," Lea said.

Scarlet set her glass back on the table. "It's called Elysium. It's a private island in the Caribbean, currently under Faulkner's control."

"Sounds neat. Maybe you could show me around?"

"I could," Scarlet said. "Except, I'm not going back."

Hawke and Lea turned to her. Lea said, "You're not?"

Scarlet shook her head and lit a cigarette. "No. I've decided after all this is over, I need to be alone, with Jack."

Camacho's face told them all that they had discussed it. "It's just how we feel," he said.

"Plus, my brother might have another mission for Bravo Troop. He's been listening in on the filthiest quarters of the internet and picking up some chatter. No details, but big bucks apparently."

Lexi rolled her eyes. "You and money."

"Go together like vodka and ice, darling, just like vodka and ice."

"You're leaving ECHO?" Ryan asked.

Scarlet leaned forward and clipped him around the ear. "Don't be so bloody stupid, boy. I just need some time away."

"Thank god for that."

"Time away from *you*," she added. "Why, will you miss me?"

"It's just that with you around, I'll have no one to insult all the time, but on the other hand, your absence will raise the team's average IQ by a full quotient."

The kick was swift and silent. The first anyone knew about it was when Ryan cried out in pain and dipped his head down as he clutched his balls.

"Oh, sorry," Scarlet said. "I was just stretching my leg. Did I hit you?"

Ryan was still gasping.

Lea glared at her. "That's not nice."

"As I've said before, I'm not essentially a nice person. Am I Ryan?" she asked. "And bear in mind, my other leg also feels like it needs a stretch."

"I would say you're the nicest of people really," he croaked. "Always very fair, and funny too."

Shrugging, Scarlet blew out some smoke. "See – he thinks I'm great."

Lea scowled at Scarlet and shook her head. "*Anyway*, after we're back on Elysium, we can take stock of the situation. Rich won't be under house arrest anymore, and we have a lot of work to do if we're going to get the place up and running again. After that, who knows?"

"I think we could all do with a break after what we're about to go through," Lexi said. "I won't be going back to Elysium, either."

A shocked silence fell over the table.

Lea spoke first. "You're not coming back either?"

She gave her head a gentle shake. "No, I need to get away from all of this. I need to empty my head completely. To be more like Ryan."

Laughter, but then she continued, more seriously. "After my parents were murdered, everything changed for me. I no longer knew what I was fighting for. The honor of the team, yes, and the paycheck, yes, but deeper than that, I was lost. When I think about Tiger still being alive, being out there somewhere, breathing the air and enjoying his life…"

"I know how you feel," Lea said. "It's how I felt about my father's killers all my life."

Lex gave a silent nod.

"Will you go after him?" Lea asked.

Now, a shallow shrug. "Maybe, maybe not. I need time to think. More than that, I need to get away and contemplate my whole life. There's a monastery I know in northern Laos. I think I will go there and consider my life, and Tiger's fate."

The mood changed again. Lea had thought that if they were successful in putting Brooke back in the White House and clearing their names, life would go on as always, only with their old HQ brought back into play. The news that neither Scarlet nor Lexi wanted to be a part of that future was like a shock of cold water over her plans.

Lea's phone rang, and she got up to take the call. As she put the phone to her ear and strolled along the riverbank, Hawke turned to the group. "Anyone else planning on moving on after we save Alex?"

Nikolai shrugged. "I am not really part of your family. You have invited me into your hearts and made me feel welcome, but I am an outsider here. I will be returning to Russia and trying to make new connections with old friends, and perhaps some of my relations."

They chatted quietly in the heat, smoking cigarettes and thinking about the best way to bring Faulkner down, then Lea returned and took her seat. "That was Orlando. We have more information about the Sukhoi jets that flew out of Vyraj yesterday."

Eager faces turned to her. "What new information?"

"The one that went to Mexico City stayed there, as we thought it would. The others went to Paris and Hong Kong. Looks like he really is going to hit more than just one city."

"But that makes three jets," Hawke said. "There were four."

Lea gave a nod. "Yeah, well the fourth one went south until the transponder cut out over Argentina."

"What the hell?" Ryan said. "So, who was on what flight?"

"Zamkov was on the southbound one," Hawke said. "Makes perfect sense."

"How?"

"Paris, Hong Kong and Mexico City all have massive populations. It stands to reason those are the locations where he wants his men to break the vials. There's nothing south of Argentina except Antarctica."

Zeke looked at him with staring eyes. "No way! You're saying Zamkov has a base on Antarctica?"

Hawke shrugged and got to his feet. "Again, it stands to reason, and it's time for us to get going. We can be in Tefé before midday and in Mexico City before dusk. Then we can end this nightmare."

"But wait," Zeke said. "We don't have the manpower to hit all those locations!"

"That's not true," Hawke said.

A sea of confused faces turned to him. "What do you mean?" the Texan asked.

Hawke gave a cautious smile. "I mean, we *do* have the manpower."

"What are you talking about?" Scarlet said. "We're on the Most Wanted list, Rich is under house arrest and Kamala is on board a Robojet flight to Antarctic hell. We have no sodding manpower at all! We'll be lucky if we can take out the Mexico City threat."

"So, what do you mean, Joe?" Lea asked.

"C'mon," he said with a wink and a grin. "I'll tell you on the plane."

CHAPTER FORTY-THREE

When Nikita Zamkov closed his eyes, he always saw snowfall. The flakes tumbled out of his memory and swirled into his imagination. He was in the forest just outside Rublyovka, chasing his sisters around the snowy pine trunks. He was watching it settle on the ground outside the apartment where he lived at university. He was skating on the ice of his private lake in the grounds of his luxury dacha.

But when he opened his eyes, he saw the rushing waters of Argentina's Iguazu Falls racing beneath his Sukhoi jet. Heat, humidity and sweat. Thick, damp air heavy with the perfume of ancient jungles and one of the most impressive waterfalls on earth.

He also saw the premium leather upholstery of the expensive private plane and the sad, tear-streaked terror on the face of Kamala Banks. She was sitting motionless with a cloth gag tied over her mouth and her hands cuffed behind her back. Once a US Secret Service agent, now a bargaining chip, should the ECHO team find their way out of the jungle and manage to track him down before he could implement Eschaton. When the supervirus was released, he would hand her over to the Dove for a few hours of pleasure before…

The thought of the power he wielded was intoxicating, and this was nothing compared with what things would be like when the last human died. This wasn't about blackmailing governments or securing more wealth for himself. This was about realizing his lifelong dream. This was about creating the world he had imagined in his mind since his childhood. A world of only sentient AI beings and him. A perfect world. A clean world. No more lies and no more filth.

As the private Sukhoi raced south, he started to relax once again, and his mind turned to his next meal of raw meat. Looking up, he saw the radiant, glowing face of Valentina Kiriyenko approaching him from the galley at the rear of the private jet. She was everything he could want in a woman. She was beautiful, she was kind.

She was a robot.

And not just any robot – she was the most advanced AI system he had ever created, leagues ahead of even Yakov. She was such a perfect a replication of the woman he had killed on that dark night in Moscow, that sometimes he wondered if he really *was* God, and he had resurrected the dead body of his girlfriend and infused her with a brand-new soul.

He turned to Yakov.

"How long until we are in Mexico City?"

"The pilot says conditions are better than expected, and we should be at our destination in less than five hours, sir."

"Good." Zamkov checked his watch and made a note of time. "The world will shortly be reborn."

He glanced at the prisoner and mulled having her gag removed. No, she was better company this way. Even bursting with fear and hatred, her eyes were still enthralling. Perhaps he would keep her alive after Eschaton, to keep her around as some kind of living memento from the old world of human flesh and blood.

Or not.

Whatever desire had to be sated could be provided by one of his AIs, after all.

Closing his eyes, he saw snow again. Maybe when all this was over, he'd move his headquarters back to Russia somewhere. He could easily see himself living in the Grand Kremlin Palace, just him and Valentina, his AI wife.

Like Adam and Eve.

THE END

AUTHOR'S NOTE

I hope you enjoyed reading *Hell's Inferno*, which I wrote in the hope of giving the ECHO team a slightly new type of adventure to pursue, as they struggle to save their kidnapped teammates and put their lives back together. I certainly enjoyed writing this one, but that's probably because I watched *Moonraker* one too many times.

Much of the AI technology in this novel might look like science fiction, but the scary thing is, most of it already exists in one form or another, and I simply embellished it to make Zamkov more dangerous. AI already writes itself, LED invisibility cloaks are already in service, and robots are already starting to walk and think for themselves.

Putting that thought out of our minds, the team's next mission – *Day of the Dead* (Joe Hawke 14) – should be arriving soon, and challenges the team with the fastest and most deadly twenty-four hours in their lives. Again, this is something slightly different and I hope you enjoy it!

And – if you enjoyed this novel or any of my other stories, please consider leaving a review on Amazon for me. It only has to be a few words – it means the world to an author and ensures further novels in the series.

JOE HAWKE WILL RETURN IN

DAY OF THE DEAD

Other Books by Rob Jones:

The Joe Hawke Series

The Vault of Poseidon (Joe Hawke #1)
Thunder God (Joe Hawke #2)
The Tomb of Eternity (Joe Hawke #3)
The Curse of Medusa (Joe Hawke #4)
Valhalla Gold (Joe Hawke #5)
The Aztec Prophecy (Joe Hawke #6)
The Secret of Atlantis (Joe Hawke #7)
The Lost City (Joe Hawke #8)
The Sword of Fire (Joe Hawke #9)
The King's Tomb (Joe Hawke #10)
Land of the Gods (Joe Hawke #11)
The Orpheus Legacy (Joe Hawke #12)
Hell's Inferno (Joe Hawke #13)

The Cairo Sloane Series

Plagues of the Seven Angels (Cairo Sloane #1)

The Avalon Adventure Series

The Hunt for Shambhala (An Avalon Adventure #1)
Treasure of Babylon (An Avalon Adventure #2)

The Raiders Series

The Raiders (The Raiders #1)

The Harry Bane Thriller Series

The Armageddon Protocol (A Harry Bane Thriller #1)

The DCI Jacob Mystery Series

The Fifth Grave (A DCI Jacob Mystery)

COMING SOON

Day of the Dead (Joe Hawke #14)

Visit Rob on the links below for all the latest news and information:

Email: robjonesnovels@gmail.com
Twitter: @AuthorRobJones
Facebook: http://bit.ly/RobJonesNovels
Website: www.robjonesnovels.com

Made in the USA
Columbia, SC
20 August 2019